# BACK TO BASICS

## AND OTHER STORIES

GILES EKINS

# CONTENTS

*For Patricia, who told me for many years to get my short stories published as a book.*
*So, here is the second volume.*

# AUTHOR'S NOTE

Some of these stories have appeared in magazines, anthologies or in larger works but are adapted here for the short story format. A few were written many years ago, and it shows.

# BACK TO BASICS

The van had been parked there all night.

About midday, the rear doors opened, a ramp dropped down and a pair of elephants came out and headed slowly down the road towards the High Street.

Sometime later, the doors opened again, and two lions strolled out, a male and a female. The male, a magnificent beast with a full, dark mane, looked across the road towards the park where some dogs roamed, but the lioness swished her tail angrily at him and, reluctantly, the lion followed her down towards the shopping arcade.

It was only when the gorillas came out and went next door to the pub that I began to think that perhaps everything was not quite as normal as it ought to be in downtown Suburbia.

I put on my jacket and went downstairs to investigate.

The van was an old, white-painted Leyland removals van and these words were painted in bright royal purple letters down the side of the van:

**Noah & Sons - Conservationists**
**By Celestial Appointment.**

There was nobody that I could see in the front cab; in fact the van looked totally deserted and neglected, covered as it was with a thick layer of road-dirt and travel-grime. If it hadn't been for the fact that elephants, lions and gorillas had all exited the van, you would assume the van had been abandoned. But unless I was hallucinating, somebody must have opened the doors to let the animals out.

Just then, the gorillas lurched out of the pub and headed to the rear of the van. I could have sworn that one of them was humming a Madonna tune. The doors opened and the gorillas, none too steadily, made their way up the ramp. I ran round to the back and up the ramp after them, but could see nothing; the gorillas seem to have completely vanished

I walked a bit further into the van and came across a black-coloured partition wall dividing the van in two. I ran my hands over the partition and pushed and heaved but the wall was solid, with none of the cracks you would expect around the edges of a door.

'Hello?' I called, hammering on the wall. 'Hello. Mr Noah?'

An oblong-shaped light appeared in the wall and an elderly man came through although no door actually seemed to open. He was tall, with white hair and beard and bright, twinkling green eyes. He wore blue overalls such as you can buy in DIY shops.

'Yes? May I help you?' he asked.

'Mr Noah?'

'Indeed so.'

'Well, I don't know how to say this without sounding like a total fruit and nutcase, but I just saw two gorillas come out of the pub and walk in here.'

'Oh dear, they haven't been a nuisance, have they? Guy can get a bit out of hand if he gets onto the vodka. I do tell him to stick to red wine but what can you do with a headstrong young gorilla, eh?'

'No, no, it's not that but... I've seen elephants and lions as well. All coming out of here.'

'Yes, it's their day out; they get a bit antsy stuck in here otherwise.'

'Is it safe? I mean, letting them out like that?'

'Yes, of course. They all know the highway code – look left, look right, look left again before crossing the road and all that.'

'I don't mean for them. I mean for people. You just can't have lions roaming about, they might attack somebody.'

'I'll have you know my lions are properly trained, taught to respect people and property, not like some of the humans you see roaming round the street these days.'

I shook my head in bemusement; this was getting way too surreal for words.

'What is this? Are you part of a circus?'

'Good heavens no, we are on a... collection mission.'

'A collection mission?'

'Yes, for the Ark 2019 Project. The Back to Basics Tour.'

'Ark? As... in... Noah's... Ark?'

'Yes, absolutely.'

I didn't know who was the most crackers, him or me. 'What are you, er... collecting?' I asked slowly.

'Come through, I'll show you.'

And most reluctantly I let him take me by the arm and lead me through the oblong light-door. Inside, the walls were lined, floor to ceiling, with hundreds and hundreds and hundreds of shiny metal drawers, each about two feet wide and three inches high.

Of the gorillas there was no sign.

To one side, there was a table set up with what I took to be a computer; although it was like no computer I had ever seen before, being shaped like a giant pile of buffalo dung with a bright screen placed in the middle. The integral keyboard was banana-shaped but without noticeable keys.

Noah sat himself down and played his fingers over the 'key-

3

board'. Lights flashed on the screen and a print-out emerged from the side of whatever it was.

'Yes, we are looking for foxes, red squirrels, Highland cattle, badgers, stoats and, if we see them, a pair of weasels, okay, but not to make a special effort otherwise.'

'Not too many Highland cattle round here,' I said.

'No, we miscalculated; the GPS system isn't working too well.'

'Global Positioning System?'

'No, God's Placement Service!'

Just then another non-door opened, and a middle-aged woman came through. Noah got to his feet, 'My wife, Joan,' he said, putting his arm around her shoulder.

'Ah, you must be Joan of Ark then,' I answered brightly. She gave me a pitying smile, the sort of smile you give to idiots and dogs.

'You're not really collecting for an Ark, are you? I mean in case there's a Great Flood?' I asked, feeling foolish even as I said it.

'Of course! Big G has just about had it with Earth. He wants to start all over again and commissioned me and my boys to build another Ark. Nearly finished, in fact.'

'But where is it? The Ark?'

Noah gave me a funny, almost crafty look. 'This is it; you're standing in it. The Ark 2008!'

'But the animals… where are the animals?'

'We've gone high-tech this time. I mean, you wouldn't believe the mess last time, hundreds and hundreds of animals cooped up in cages for forty days and nights.'

'The smell,' interjected Joan.' The smell was simply over-powering.'

'And not only that, I don't know how many species the tigers made extinct when they escaped from their pens and starting eating things.'

'And that huge Ark was so unmanageable.'

'Yes, we were trying to get to Florida. We were going to set up what you'd call a theme park there, but we ended up on Mt Ararat."

'Florida?'

'Yes. Of course we didn't call it Florida back in those days, it was called Barzaccalajahar.'

Definitely loony tunes, I thought.

I looked round the 'Ark' again, searching for signs of any animals, but nothing – not even a mouse dropping.

'But… where are the animals?' I asked again.

'As I told you, we've gone hi-tech,' answered Noah. 'Any animal which is in the programme passes through the processing screen,' and he patted the partition wall. 'It's what we call an ACTIMORASTIFLAZ screen. I couldn't possibly begin to tell you what the acronym ACTIMORASTIFLAZ stands for, but in essence it reduces the subject to basic DNA genes which are then stored on a sort of floppy disk,' and Noah opened what looked like a microwave oven mounted at the side of his desk and pulled out two shiny metallic strips the size and thickness of a credit card. 'This is Guy and this is Geraldine, the gorillas.' He ran his fingers along the rows of drawers, opened one and slid the cards inside. A purplish glow emanated from the drawer.

'But I passed through the screen,' I said. 'Why wasn't I reduced to a Visa Platinum card?'

'Ah now, there you have it. Humans aren't in the programme.'

'Not in the programme?' I asked, with a sense of growing unease.

'No, 'fraid not. the Boss has got utterly fed up with humans, biggest mistake he ever made, he says. What with endless wars and global warming and the destruction of the rainforests, the pollution of the seas, Big G has had enough. Hence the Back to Basics Tour. Humans, I'm afraid, are going to become extinct.'

'And not a moment too soon,' added Joan.

'Humans and flies!'

'And fruit bats, nasty messy things.'

'But... but what about you two? Aren't you humans? I enquired.

'Good heavens, no!'

'God forbid!'

'We are solabnods.'

'And proud of it.'

'Solabnods?'

'From the planet Solabno, in the Malaknid Galaxy, 179,000,000,000,000,000 and 2 light years away.

'Took us over a week to get here, but the traffic was so heavy around Andromeda.'

Just then a light started flashing on the dung-computer.

'Noah, you've got G mail,' said Joan.

'G mail?' I asked,

'Yes, like email,' she responded, 'but it's Yehovah.com rather than yahoo.com. A much more powerful server. What is it, dear?' Joan asked.

'Big G wants us to wrap things up immediately. Seems as though that storm front is moving rather quicker than antici- pated, something to do with solar winds, apparently.'


Noah came over to me and shook my hand. 'Very nice to meet you, old chap, but I rather doubt we shall be meeting again.'

'Yes, lovely to see you,' echoed Joan, insincerity dripping off her like water off a drowned fruit-bat.

Noah ushered me outside.

It was raining.

Raining rather heavily!

# THE LEMONADE STALL

*Some of what follows did happen.*
*Meerut. Northern India, 10 May 1857*

The late afternoon sun beats down mercilessly on the brightly coloured awnings of the Meerut bazaar, etching deep shadows into the doorways and twisting myriad alleys of the bazaar as spear-sharp shards of blinding light suddenly sear back from the whitewashed walls, a dazzling assault of darkest shadow and piercing brightness.

A distant murmuration, a thrumming like an oncoming train approaching the station, the noise undulates, and surges and angry, enraged screams begin to echo through the streets and lanes, a swelling of hatred, of anger and of a fearful bloodlust. In the far distance, an orange glow permeates the sky as a swirling pillar of smoke blackens it.

Terrified, his face blanched in terror, a young British soldier runs for his life, pursued by the hate-fuelled mob shouting their hatred as they chase the Dragoon through the narrow alleys and streets of the bazaar. The screams of hate cascade into his ears and fear seizes his pounding heart as they chase him down. '*Mat karo, Mat karo, Siphai jai,*' they yell. Kill! Kill!

'Help! Help me!' he screams in turn, his cries drowned out by the mob closing down on his heels.

The narrow lanes are busy now with off-duty sepoys and sowars, stall vendors hawking their wares, sari-clad *bibis* with little naked *chicos* about their skirts who yell and scream at the young Dragoon Guard as he runs for his life... runs as if all the banshees of hell were at his heels. His bursting lungs gasp for air in the hot, humid, dust-laden air, the fetid, windless alleys redolent with the stench of urine, human shit and cattle dung, of rich spices and the smoke from countless small cooking braziers.

His shako flies from his head to be kicked aside by the chanting, rioting, angry mob, yelling and screaming incoherently, seeing only their terrified prey before them, unmindful of anything except the burning need to kill the hated *gora-log,* the instincts of the mob overriding all else. *Hatya! Hatya. Hatya.* Kill, kill, kill.

Imagine, if you can, his terror as he flees through the narrow, snaking lanes and alleys, his heart pounding, his lung burning, most likely with no idea why the pursuing mob are so determined to kill him; probably many of the chasing horde do not know why, either, being simply caught up in the maelstrom of mob hysteria.

A native woman clad in a rich green sari spits at him and curses as the soldier runs by. Another tries to trip him. He avoids the outstretched foot but in doing so he stumbles, his arms windmilling as he tries to keep his balance, but he is slowed and the mob, seeing the stumble, roar with exultation, knowing their prey is falling ever closer. Desperately, he pushes his aching legs on, knowing that another slip or stumble will cost him his life.

Just then, a small girl runs out from a shop doorway, her mother in pursuit. The child runs straight in front of the fleeing soldier. He tries to avoid her, but his iron-cleated boot catches her on the shin and, with a yelp of pain, she falls to the ground and her mother is unable to reach her before she is trampled beneath the feet of the pursuing mob. With a wail of distress, the *chico's* mother can only watch in horror as the little girl is crushed into the hard-beaten earth of the bazaar. Once the rampaging mob is past, she cradles the broken body of her daughter to her breast and keens in anguish. This will not be the first death this day.

The soldier runs on but he is tiring. The indolent regime in the Meerut cantonment is not conducive to fitness and athleticism; a white private soldier did not draw his own water, did not cook his own meals, did not wash his own clothes, was shaved as he lay in his bed and spent the days in boredom and idleness in the shade of his barracks block, venturing out only when the baking Indian sun was sinking, when the heat of the day was dissipating, when all passions should have evaporated under the remorseless heat.

The young Dragoon is tiring fast and the pursuit behind is relentless, bearing down ever closer, a fluid, flowing horde of hate and bloodlust. He stumbles one last time and crashes into a lemonade stall, sending a score of bottles and glasses cascading to the ground. Holding his hip in pain, he limps on, but he is doomed. The front runners of the mob, a dozen or so regimental sepoys in jackets and cross belts, are spurred on by the Dragoon's collision and seize him, bearing him up as he thrashes and flails. They yell incoherently in triumph and bloodlust and he is hurled down onto the table of the lemonade stall and held by his arms and legs as others seize up the broken bottles and stab and slash at the screaming soldier, slashing at his face and eyes, blood streaking in torrents to mingle with the lemonade foam.

'*Angreji cala kutte ko mauta.*' Death to the English running dog. '*Hatya, hatya, hatya.*' Kill. Kill !

Yet more bottles are smashed as the milling rioters seize the razor-sharp shards to stab at his genitals and stomach. He writhes and screams in agony as the bloodied bottle shards rise and stab, rise and stab, rise and stab, slashing and slicing, mutilating him beyond recognition. Yet still he screams and thrashes, his entire body a blood-drenched nightmare, his uniform hacked to shreds, his flesh rent to bloodied scraps. A rope is then looped about his neck and he is hoisted up to a beam, the blood draining and pouring from his multitude of wounds as he thrashes and twists on the rope's end, his face a bloody, flesh-stripped mask, one pulped eye dangling by an ocular thread. Even as he hangs there, now thankfully on the point of death, the mob continues to hack and slash at his body as it twists this way and that.

It is only when there are no more bottles to smash that the bloodlust eases, evaporating as quickly as it has arisen for many of the rioters. As if suddenly ashamed of their actions, many of the bloody-handed mob begin to slink away, suddenly fearful that retribution must surely follow; retribution that will be relentless and severe and many now fear they will be brought to summary justice on the gallows of the British.

Others, the ringleaders, mostly sepoys, yell and shout their exultation, urging the remaining mob to commit more murder, more killings.

'See, brothers, it is done. Death to the British, death to the British, already the sahibs are fleeing, running like dogs to the sea. We will destroy them all, it is foretold, it is written, we will drive them from the beloved land. Come brothers, to the white town, free your shackles. Kill. Kill the running dogs, the white devils. Death. Death. Death. Death to the *gora-log*.'

As the last of the murderous rioters move on, the proprietor of the lemonade stall cautiously eases out from his hiding place at the rear of the stall, prudently keeping out of the way as the deadly riot rampaged through the streets. Standing amid the rivers of blood and lemonade, the gore-slicked glass knives, the smashed chairs, the broken bottles and glasses, BGP Joshi surveys the ruin of his business. At best, it was a precarious enterprise, barely covering the cost of the lemons, (he only ever used the best and freshest, most expensive lemons) sugar and boiled water, the rent on the corner premises and the repayment to Gobinda, the *sahukara*, the usurious moneylender from whom he borrowed many lakh to start up the stall. BGP Joshi has no chance whatever of restocking his stall, replacing the broken bottles and glasses; no chance whatsoever of paying his rent, or of satisfying the rapacious moneylender, or of putting food on the table for his family. He is ruined – ruined beyond the devastation of his business, utterly ruined. His debts will follow him to his grave; follow him to his children's children and beyond.

Sadly, he turns to the swaying body of the murdered soldier and briefly takes hold of his bloody hand, as if to comfort him. *'Gariba, gariba larake.'* Poor, poor boy. He can see that the dead soldier was little more than a youth. BGP Joshi likes the *Angreji, Angreji sainikom*, the English and the English soldiers. The English memsahibs are good customers, as are the soldiers, but he knows that as well as his ruination, the avenging soldiers will assume him to be complicit in the killing. After all, the soldier has been hacked to death on his doorstep, so no questions would be asked as to his guilt or not, for surely, by all the gods, the *Angreji* will hang him, hoist him high to choke out his last on the gallows' crossbeam.

(I do not know the identity of the soldier so brutally killed that day. As much as I have read histories of the Indian Mutiny – or Indian Rebellion depending on your point of view – or visited websites, I can find no reference to give me his name. He deserves to be named; he was amongst the first of those who died in the bloody events of the mutiny; at the very least he should be remembered by name.)

As the realisation of the inevitable retribution to follow strikes him, BGP Joshi quickly runs back inside the tiny smoke-filled rooms in which he lives with his wife Amishi, his son Gopal and daughter Lakshaki.

'Quickly, woman!' he shouts to his wife, as she squats beside a small fire cooking chapattis and lentils. 'Gather everything,

everything we can carry. We must go now. Now! Before the soldiers come and hang me.'

'Go? Go, husband? Why must we go?'

'Not to argue, just do as told, collect everything that we can carry, we must go to Agra, to stay with second cousin. No time to lose. Quickly. *Jildi, jildi.*'

Amishi does not argue further. Quickly and efficiently, she gathers together their mediocre possessions. Needing to take the cooking utensils, she plucks them from the fire, burning her hands as she does so, then squats and urinates to douse the fire. She wraps such clothes as they have into a large bundle that she will carry on her head and tells her daughter to put any food and cooking ghee into a large earthenware bowl which she will have to carry, as BGP flusters and interferes, creating confusion and turmoil, wringing his hands in anguish and urging greater speed whilst picking up objects, putting them down again before holding them indecisively, nodding his head from side to side in agitation.

'Gopal. Where is Gopal?' he suddenly asks, only just realising that the boy is not there, looking around to every corner as if expecting the boy to magically appear,

'Gopal? He went to see his friend Sanjay.'

'What for he sees Sanjay? His place is here, working, for what else does a man have sons but to follow him in his business?

'We must wait for him to come back.'

'No, no waiting. Soldiers will come any minute, any moment now and hang me for the poor boy, even though I do nothing, was not there, was here, but angry soldiers will not listen, angry soldiers never listen, only hanging and killing, maybe hanging Gopal, too.'

'Gopal? He is just a boy.'

'Soldiers not caring, only caring for hanging and killing. We go. Now! Leave message for Gopal at Laxman's shop across the way, he is to follow us on road to Agra. Now, we go. Lakshaki, come. Come. Now!'

And BGP Joshi hurries out, barely glancing at the body of the murdered soldier still hanging there as no one else dared approach or take him down for fear of retribution. Fearfully, Amishi and Lakshaki, with eyes downcast, skirt the body and follow on behind BGP Joshi as he scuttles through the alleys towards the outskirts of the town and the road to Agra. Burdened by their heavy loads, mother and daughter struggle to keep up with the fleeing Joshi, who carries only a gaudy plaster effigy of the Hindu god Vishnu, the Protector.

(Did Gopal ever catch up with his family? I do not know. I would like to think so, but most probably not, he was most likely caught up in the mayhem which follows. BGP Joshi, Amishi and Lakshaki must leave us now, not to return)

Behind them, the town of Meerut erupts into an orgy of massacre, looting, rape, killing, mutiny and rebellion.

The Indian Mutiny had begun.

# BROTHERS

On a wintry December's night in the year 1542, shivering monks scurried from their dormitory to the side door of the church as a bitter, icy wind sliced through the arches of the cloisters. It was 2am, the hour of the Matins prayers and the monks, blue with cold, lined up two by two, waiting for the sub prior to open the door. It was not heated inside the church but at least inside, they would be protected from the bitter wind.

It was singularly unusual for there to be no direct access from the monks' first floor dormitory to the body of the church. Most monasteries had a night stair leading to the west nave, but here, the monks came down via a staircase to the far corner of the cloisters, which, although roofed over, were open at the sides, open to the chilling icy wind and driven rain and sleet.

Icicles hung in glistening fangs from the eaves and gutters of the cloisters; an owl hooted in triumph as it swooped down on a mouse or vole scurrying through the winter-barren cloister gardens before soaring over the roof of the cloisters and up to its nest in the belfry tower. Most of the monks were too cold and miserable to notice, as they huddled into their thin woollen tunics, the hoods of their scapulars wrapped tightly about their heads, stamping their sandaled feet in a vain attempt to keep warm,

The monastery, dedicated to St Severianus, was in fact extremely poor. St Severianus was a minor saint, not even a martyr and the monastery itself held little in the way of significant religious relics that were necessary to attract wealthy paying pilgrims. There were no nails from the Crucifixion, no authenticated splinters of wood from the True Cross, no bones from any of the apostles or important saints, not a shred of desiccated skin from the flayed St Bartholomew or even a fingernail cutting from St Severianus himself. There was no rich patron hoping to buy his place in heaven and the monks themselves mostly came from poor families, third or fourth sons sent to the care of the monastery so as to reduce the number of mouths to feed.

The abbot, Brother Anselm, believed that mortification of the flesh was the way for monks to achieve salvation. Not the mortification of his own flesh, of course, of which there was an amplitude, but that of the brothers and so he declined to heat any of the monastery rooms, apart from, obviously, his own quarters.

As they had done for the past twenty-seven years, Brother Francis and Brother Joseph lined up side by side. They did not speak. None of the monks spoke, for theirs was a silent order and on entering, they had all taken vows of obedience, poverty, chastity and silence. The only human voice they heard would be that of the lector entrusted with the reading of prayers or lessons. Instructions for the daily routine of the monastery were given by signs or written orders.

However, notwithstanding their vows of silence, a visceral loathing and hatred between Francis and Joseph was clearly evident, with looks and body language of such intense virulence that it seemed to shroud them in a personal mist of hate. Despite their decades of bitter enmity, not a word or a voice raised in anger had passed between them, but this silent loathing did nothing to lower the intensity of their hatred for each other;

rather, it raised it, there being no outlet by which they could communicate or resolve their differences.

Suddenly, Brother Joseph stood up tall. His head jerked back as his eyes rolled up through their sockets and he swayed on his feet, like a tall tree awaiting the final stroke of the axe to bring it crashing down. His legs crumpled beneath him and he fell in a dead faint to the floor, crashing into Brother Saviour behind him. The startled monks gathered around their stricken brother in consternation before Brother Francis took charge of the situation, pushing the bewildered brethren away as they hovered over Joseph like black carrion crows.

By signs and gestures, he managed to get four of the monks to carry Joseph to the infirmary, followed at a distance by Brother John, the elderly infirmarian. Once inside the infirmary Francis, without seeking approval, lit a fire. The fire did little to heat the frigid room, but the flames did give off a cheery orange glow, belying the cold. The only other occupant of the infirmary was Brother Paul, who was dying but did not seem to realise that fact and was taking his time about it.

By candlelight, Brother John examined Joseph's body for plague buboes – red swellings, sure sign of the dreaded Black Death, sent by God as punishment for sin – but to everyone's relief he was clear. The plague could totally decimate a closed community such as the monastery.

Then Brother John bled Joseph. Using a none-too-clean knife, he opened a vein in Joseph's forearm and collected blood in a wooden chalice, before washing the incision with red wine and binding the arm with a cloth bandage. He sniffed at the blood, dipped a finger in it and tasted it on the tip of his tongue, grimacing as he did so.

Medieval medical belief held that disease or illness was caused by an imbalance in the four bodily humours, i.e., blood, phlegm, black bile and yellow bile and that blood-letting could correct the imbalance. Also, it was not understood that blood circulated throughout the body; rather it was believed that blood was static and could become stagnant if not regularly drained.

However, the bleeding of Brother Joseph seemed to have little effect. He was still unconscious, in a high fever, alternatively sweating profusely or shivering with cold.

Brother John shrugged. Despite his position as infirmarian, he had little medical knowledge. His position had been granted by the abbot as a reward for concealing some very un-abbot like indiscretions and he now left the infirmary, content to let Francis do what little he could for Joseph.

Brother Francis was the monastery herbalist and it was his responsibility to tend to the herb garden which housed dozens of different herbs, some of which were sent to the kitchen, but most of which were collected and dried for medicinal purposes.

Joseph was now shivering violently, so Francis covered him with three or four thin blankets, all that were available in the infirmary, before hurrying to the dormitory to fetch his own blanket to cover the stricken monk.

From the kitchen he brought a bowl of warm water and gently wiped away the sweat from Joseph's face and body. He sat there by his side, continually wiping him until it was time for Lauds, the early morning service.

He had little time before Prime, the next service, but even so, he collected four bricks from a collapsed garden wall, wrapped them in a cloth and placed them in a tub of boiling water. Once they were heated, he placed the hot bricks about Joseph's shivering body, to his feet, his chest and sides and then hurried to the church for the service.

After Prime, Francis hurried back to tend to Joseph, who still lay in a high fever, his head burning to the touch as he swam in and out of consciousness, mumbling incoherently. Francis bathed him again in warm water, reheated the warming bricks, built up the fire again and burned some sprigs of dried rosemary and thyme to drive away noxious airs which, in his mind, were the real cause of diseases. Then he placed a cap with sachets of lavender sewn inside on Joseph's head, to ease the headache.

In the nearby bed, Brother Paul still lay dying, his laboured breath echoing around the dismal infirmary.

There was time before the next service for Francis to prepare a decoction to reduce Joseph's fever. In the herbarium, he ground coriander seeds with a mortar and pestle and added dried yarrow and chamomile leaves together with powdered angelica root, before boiling them in water for a few minutes. He then strained the liquid through a gauze cloth and allowed it to cool.

Holding his head up from the pillow, Francis gently drip fed the decoction into Joseph's mouth. He spluttered and spat much of the liquid out but some was swallowed. Before going to Terce prayers, Francis went to the kitchen and put some lean beef, butter, a clove, two small onions and salt into a pot of water and set it on a stove to slow-simmer. After the service, he scooped away the scum and fat from the surface and left it simmering again so that the meat was completely rendered down.

Shortly afterwards, Brother Paul finally realised that he was dying and duly obliged. After a service for the dead, he was wrapped in his shroud and buried in the monastery cemetery.

After Nones, the afternoon service, Francis fed small spoonfuls of the beef tea to Joseph, the only food he could take down, as the flax seed porridge with honey that Francis prepared had proved indigestible.

And so this routine continued for the next two days and nights until Joseph's fever finally broke. In that time Francis slept but little. When not at prayer, he was devotedly at Joseph's bedside, wiping him down with warm water, cleaning him when he fouled himself and feeding him the herbal decoction and beef tea. At last, very weak, Joseph rose from his bed and, supported by Francis, made his way back to the dormitory. At no time did he look at Francis or acknowledge the dedicated care his brother had given him, for they were indeed true brothers, brothers of the womb, sent to the monastery as oblates when they were seven and five respectively, their hatred emanating from childhood quarrels long forgotten; only the poisonous animosity remained.

As they had done for the past twenty-seven years, Brother Francis and Brother Joseph lined up side by side, with looks and body language of such intense virulence that it seemed to shroud them in a personal mist of hate, any acknowledgment of fraternal bond or obligation once again abandoned.

# CALL ME RUBY

'Call me Ruby,' he said, big-toothed smile spreading all across his florid, cherubic face, a large gold tooth twinkling like an early morning sunburst. Katie and I looked at each other. *Ruby?* we thought. How can you trust a house agent who calls himself Ruby? 'My name is actually Rueben, Rueben Ball,' he explained, 'but everybody has called me Ruby ever since I was no taller than a grasshopper on your knee.'

We might have called him Ruby to his face, and his proper name might be Rueben Ball, but privately we always called him Rubber Ball, because that is exactly what he was like. No more than five foot two inches tall, he was equally as rotund, like Tweedle-dum and Tweedle-dee rolled into one. And he did not walk, he bounced, as if he has springs on the balls of his feet – boing-boing-boing. His suit was a violent yellow check, he wore a pink shirt with frilly cuffs and sported a red-spotted bow tie that revolved whenever he pressed a concealed switch in his pockets.

First impressions did not impress.

Katie and I were looking for a house. We had been together for almost eighteen months, renting a small (as in tiny) apartment next door to an undertaker (which did have the advantage of quiet neighbours) and we had finally decided to get married, set up home, take on mortgages we couldn't afford, have the statistical 2.4 kids, the whole marital shebang, arguments optional.

We'd been walking along the High Street, looking at the property details in the estate agents window but unable to find anything we liked. Correction: we could find lots of houses we liked but could find nothing we liked at a price we could afford and, to be perfectly honest, Katie wanted a mansion on a cottage budget, whereas I would be quite content with a small cottage on a large tent budget.

It was Ruby's sign which made us actually walk into his office. Positioned above the door, it proclaimed, *Rueben Ball, The Best Move of All* and his logo was a house shaped like a ball, complete with windows and a door, drawn to look as though it was moving. We laughed, and walked in, even though none of the properties on display were in our price range.

'Call me Ruby,' he said again, 'Ruby Ball, one size fits all. So, my dears, you are looking for a property, of course you are looking for property, why else would you darken my windows? Do we look as though we sell the priceless antiquities of ancient Bubblegum? No, of course not, you want a house, a very-table mansion, fitful for a king.' He bounced again, several chins wobbling in unison as he laughed at his own jokes. Jokes?

Katie explained what we (she) was looking for.

'On no, dreary me, dreary me. You have a time machine maybe?'

*Time machine?* Katie looked blank but I grasped his meaning.

'You mean that, say, ten, fifteen years ago we could have bought what we want with the money we have available, but not now.'

'Exfactly! Exfactly! But with inflution, spiralling property prices!' Ruby shrugged and whole his body wobbled like jelly in an earthquake. 'But let us see, let us see, Ruby can always find a bargain – but not for free-hee.'

21

We looked at each other again and Kate rolled her eyes in derision. Ruby saw but pretended not to, probably used to it.

His fingers, as plump as a pound of thick pork sausages, played over his computer keyboard with surprising dexterity as he sang to himself 'Eerie, merey, dreary me. Eerie, merey, dreary me,' a large ruby ring on his pinkie finger flashing like a beacon under the light from his desk lamp. 'Now this is a little thing which might interest you, oh yes. A bye-joe little town house in Eastwick, on Elm Street – with absolubely no dark horses at night. It will need a little bit of work, a lady's eye for decoration, and a dab hand with a paint brush. It is slightly over your budget, but I am sure that Ruby can negotiate it down for you.'

His agile fingers raced across the keyboard and an asthmatic printer began to chatter away to itself, printing out details of the bye-joe little house on Elm Street.

We consulted, Katie and I; the price, if it could be negotiated down a bit – well more than a bit – could just about be affordable.

'Let us go and inspectulate', Ruby said. 'Ruby recommends immediate inspectulation, strike whilst the irons are shot, thyme and sage wait for no man.'

He drove us out to inspectulate, fitting himself with easy grace into a sport-tuned Saab and driving with a skill you would not believe possible as he wove in and out of the traffic and got us to the house in short time. *A little bit of work*, he said? Apart from the fact that Kate hated it on sight, the master bedroom was so small you had to shuffle sideways to get around the bed.

'Not very commodious, not combodious at all,' Ruby sang, 'but there again, neither are you, hoo-hoo.'

The bathroom was a nightmare, despite what Ruby had said (I don't think Katie ever caught on to the *Nightmare on Elm Street* reference). It had been painted black, utterly and completely black, walls, floor, ceiling, bathtub, washbasin, toilet, toilet seat, taps, handles – everything. Even the toilet paper was black. We politely declined to look around any further.

'No matters, no matters, if at thirst you don't succeed, give up. No, dreary me, that's not at all right. Ruby will not be defeated; Ruby has never been defeated. Defeat is not my middle name. We take the noble steed back to Ruby's office and the search for the mouldy gruel will continue.'

Property number two, in Vernon Street, was, if at all possible, even worse. It was an end terrace house, bow-fronted with a weed-encrusted garden that had not seen a spade or lawn mower since before the Boer War. OK, that could soon remedied with a couple of weekends of sweat and hard labour. What could not be sorted, even with an army of builders, painters, plumbers, decorators, electricians, pest exterminator and a disinfection squad, was that the house was in a state of terminal dereliction, as the previous owner, a widow of ninety-three, had not maintained the property since the death of her husband in 1952. The widow herself had died some time previously and had not been found for many months. She had died without heirs and after her death the house had been occupied by squatters, who had stripped out every single fitting they could and, on being evicted, had smashed up any fitting that could not be ripped out and sold. Toilet facilities seemed to be wherever the squatters had felt like it (pun not intended).

Apart from that, the house seemed to be built on a fault line and had subsided by several inches, creating cracks through the walls through which you could observe the traffic and passers-by on the street outside.

Ruby looked chastened, at least for all of two minutes. 'Not to worry, worry never caught a dragon by the tail, worry should be posted in the mail. Ha, Ruby never worries, he never bites his nails, Ruby, Ruby never ever fails.'

When it was pointed out to him that he had in fact failed, he bounced about again on his rubberised feet. 'Time is not of the easement, am I not wrong? Oh no, drearie me, Ruby will find you the perfect manse, a cosy retreat for two, then perhaps to be three or four or more?'

My confidence in Ruby was now about as shaky as the foundations of No 56 Vermin Street – sorry, Vernon Street.

Strangely enough, if anything, Katie's confidence in Ruby seemed to be growing. To her, his inane jokes and malapropisms bordered on comic genius, and to be fair, the next properties Ruby showed were better. Although not much... I have to wonder whether he showed those horrors as a sort of joke; certainly, Katie seemed to find it hilarious.

First impressions had not impressed, neither had the third or fourth.

The next two properties he showed were not as bad, but that was only by comparison. The first property was a small cottage that had once been a farm cottage but had now been swallowed by the relentless outward march of the town. Set back from the road by a large front garden with a bird bath and two apple trees, it contained two small bedrooms, (*compact beejoo* was Ruby's description) with low ceilings, pretty timber beams designed specifically to crack your skull every time you stood up (although not a problem for Ruby), a tidy kitchen extension built onto the rear with nice views of an old outhouse, a surprisingly large living/dining room and a small rear garden. I thought it had potential, so of course Katie hated it and hated me for liking it.

The next house was another free-standing, bow-fronted house, in need of some repairs and modernization, the only trouble being that it stood at the top of a hill so steep that come winter snow or ice fall, you'd need to be Sherpa Tensing to reach it. I doubted if even a Land Rover could make it. Ruby's Saab strove mightily in first gear to get to the top and we rapidly concluded that the house was only fit for mountain goats and gave it a miss. How anybody managed to build it remains a mystery.

I then had to go to Frankfurt on business for a few days and Katie and I decided that she should carry on looking. I suggested she try another agent, but she would not hear of it. 'I'm sure

Ruby will find exactly what we're looking for, we just have to give him time. I mean, as he says, time is not of the easement.'

I came back from Germany after eight days, a day earlier than I had intended, but the deal was finalized and signed quicker than anticipated.

Katie was not in the apartment when I got back, and it was quite late in the evening when she finally did come home. 'Oh!' she said, as though surprised to find me there. 'I thought you were in Germany?'

'I was, but we finished early. I tried to call but you didn't answer.'

'I've been busy. I found a house, the perfect house. Ideal.'

'That's great. Where?'

'It's Ruby's house. I'm moving in with him. I've only come back to pack my things.' And with that, she left.

I suppose you could say it was, after all, The Best Move of All.

At least for me it was.

# LOOKING GOOD IN A PAUL
## SMITH SUIT

Barry Nicholls read the email again, utterly convinced that it was genuine.

*From: Akintola Kabira<AKabira@yahoo.com*

*Dear Sir,*

*ASSISTANCE REQUIRED FOR ACQUISITION OF ESTATE*

*I write to inform you of my desire to acquire estates or landed properties in your country on behalf of the Director of Contracts and Finance Allocations for the Federal Ministry of Oil and Petroleum in Nigeria . Considering his very strategic and influential position, he would want the transaction to be as strictly confidential as possible and wants his identity to remain undisclosed until the completion of the business. Hence the desire for an overseas agent. After enquiry, I have been given your name as an upright and honest businessman and instructed by my principal to enquire whether you would act in the capacity to actualise this transaction.*

*The deal, in brief, is that the funds that we wish to transfer are presently in a coded account in the Central Bank of Nigeria and we need your assistance to transfer the funds to a convenient bank in your country. For this you will be considered to have executed a contract with the Federal Government of Nigeria in the contract sum of $26,400,000 of which your share will be 10% - 5% will be set aside for expenses.*

*As soon as payment is effected and the amount mentioned is successfully transferred into your account, we intend to use our share to purchase real estate abroad, for this you will also be asked to act as our agent on commission.*

*In the light of this I would like you to forward to me the following information:*

*1. Your company name and address, if not a registered company, please establish same as Federal funds cannot be transferred to individuals.*
*2. Your personal fax and telephone number.*
*You are requested to communicate your acceptance of this proposal through my above stated email after which we shall discuss in detail the modalities of the transaction.*

*Yours faithfully*
*Akintola Kabira.*

Of course, Barry knew that there were lots of scams, especially from Nigeria – 419 scams, they were called – but there was no way he was going to be caught like that, was there?

The real scams involved such ridiculous amounts of money that they were obviously bogus, but this one, this one really sounded genuine. And what was the risk? He was not being asked to put any money up front, simply act as the middle man, the expeditor, and pick up $2,400,000 for his trouble, which converts to £1,607,224.13. Say that again – one million, six hundred and seven thousand, two hundred and twenty-four pounds. All he had to do was expedite the transfer of funds from Nigeria to a bank account in England. Simple!

*From: <BNicholls@hotmail.com*
*I accept, my details are...*

He wasn't going to use his own personal bank account, of course, he wasn't that naïve, but for £100 he could set up a company and call it Nicholls Inc. He liked the sound of that.

On his way to the bank to set up a dedicated account, he passed by the Porsche showroom. The black Porsche Boxster gleamed, polished to an inch of its life. That's going to be mine, said Barry to himself.

*From: <BNicholls@hotmail.com*
*As requested, I have now established the dedicated company account at Barclay's Bank, account no.......*

*From: Akintola Kabira<AKabira@yahoo.com*
*Dear Mr Nicholls,*

*Thank you for the details of the bank account, please establish me as a signatory on the company account, as per Federal law. This is proce-dure only.*

*A letter of confirmation from the Central Bank of Nigeria (CBN)*

*confirming that the sum of $26,400,000 will be transferred to the new
account has today been sent by registered post.*

It's happening, Barry thought exultantly, it's really happening!
    Two days later, he received another email.

*From: Akintola Kabira <AKabira@yahoo.com*

*Dear Barry,*
*The CBN require a transaction fee of $10,000, under CBN regulations
this has to be forwarded by the receiving agent. This is standard proce-
dure and the amount will of course be deducted from the 5% which we
have allocated against expenses*

Obviously, there are going to be expenses, Barry reasoned, which
is why the 5% – $1,320,000 – had been set aside. He arranged for
the transfer of funds from his personal account to the new dedicated company account and on to a numbered account in
Nigeria.
    The letter from the Central Bank of Nigeria, confirming the
transfer, came in the next morning. Barry read it a dozen times;
caressing the crisp white paper embossed with the logo of the
bank and the heavy red wax seal affixed to the bottom of the
letter, trying to decipher the scrawling signature of the Executive
Manager, Dr. Joseph Ebong. He held the letter to his nose,
smelling it, the heady scent of money.
    *Yes!* thought Barry and went to drool over his Porsche again.
    Anticipating his new wealth, he rang the credit card
company and increased his limit. He would be paying it all off
soon enough. He then booked a holiday in Phuket – first class

airfares, 5-star hotels, nothing but the best from now on. He bought a new stereo, a top-of-the-range DVD home entertainment centre and celebrated with a meal and a bottle of very expensive claret at Giorgio's, the most exclusive restaurant in town.

He was going to be seriously rich and there was no way he was going to tell Angela, his ex-wife – she would bleed him dry if she knew he had that sort of money.

To mark his forthcoming riches, he next bought a new suit from Paul Smith, together with fifteen stylish shirts to be worn open-necked with the suit. Dressed in his new suit and feeling like a million dollars – make that a million pounds – he called in at the Porsche showroom again. He ran his fingers lasciviously along the sweeping bodywork, – 'buy me,' the gleaming black Boxster seemed to whisper – 'buy me now, make me yours.' Unable to resist, Barry put down the deposit and established monthly credit arrangements until he could pay off the balance in full.

When he got back home, there was another email waiting.

*From:Akintola Kabira <AKabira@yahoo.com*

*Dear Barry,*
*We have encountered a minor difficulty – it seems that the CBN Regulator is asking for commission on the transaction, this is nothing short of blackmail, but unfortunately this is how things work in Nigeria. From the 5% allocated for expenses, please transfer the sum of $25,000, without this the transaction will fail… urgent…*

Although a bit taken aback by this latest demand, Barry could see the reasoning behind it. Nigeria was listed as one of the two most corrupt countries in the world by Transparency

International, the world watch-dog on corruption, so when he thought about it, he was not really surprised that bank officials would try and skim off some of the money.

And it was not as though it was going to come out of his share of the deal. He would have to take out a loan for this, but there was plenty of equity on his apartment and he would be paying it back – and more, much more – very soon. anyway. The loan agreed, Barry telexed the transfer to the account in Nigeria, sure that the $26,400,000 would be transferred very soon.

As he slowly cruised down the High Street in the black Porsche Boxster, he could not help but notice the admiring looks that came his way. This is the life, he thought, and this is only the beginning.


*From:Akintola Kabira <AKabira@yahoo.com*

*Dear Barry,*

*It saddens and greatly embarrasses to once again have to approach you in this matter. Dr Ebong, the Executive Manager of CBN, is now insisting upon his 'commission'. Of course, as a more important offi-cial, his commission must be greater than the Regulator, hence $30,000.*

*I am assured that once the money is paid, he will release the transfer of the funds. In order to speed things, my principal has taken a short term loan against his mother's house and I have sold my wife's jewellery so the transfer will take place with immediate effect, but you must urgently transfer the $30,000 from the expenses fund to cover our loss. My friend, I am ashamed to beg of you like this, but we are so close to the realisation of our dream.*

Taking another loan against his apartment, Barry reluctantly sent off the money – after all, it would be silly to have come so far and stop now.

*From:Akintola Kabira <AKabira@yahoo.com*

*Great news, the transfer has now been approved by the Federal Ministry of Finance and National Economy.*
*However, as it is deemed you have contracted work for the Federal Government, by law, all companies dealing with the Federal Government must have assets of $100,000 in their bank in order to demonstrate fiscal probity, please arrange to place $100,000 in the company account. Do NOT send the money to Nigeria but fax a bank statement confirming the worth of the company. On receipt, the transfer of funds will take place immediately...*

*My very good friend, at last we are there. .*

Barry never heard from Akintola Kabira again. When he checked the account to see whether the $26,400,000 had been transferred, he found his account empty, the $100,000 had gone. The police could do nothing, nor could the bank and the Nigerian Embassy refused to comment.

The Porsche was repossessed, and Barry was forced to sell his apartment to pay off the loans. He was homeless and destitute – but he still looked good in the Paul Smith suit and open-neck shirt.

# A HERO OF THE TOWN ONCE MORE
## A YORKSHIRE TOWN, CIRCA 1955.

PC Percy Copper was a hero about town. Or so he still believed. Not so long ago he had foiled an armed bank robbery, losing the little finger of his left hand from a shotgun blast in the process. He had been feted in the press, received a commendation from the Chief Constable and everyone in the squad room had been happy to shake his hand or pat him on the back.

But fame is a transient thing, fleeting and ephemeral, a fickle mistress and now he was simply back to where he had been just a few short weeks ago, a humble copper walking his beat. And none too happy about it.

Judy Dennison, a twelve-year-old schoolgirl, had been attacked on her way home after a Girl Guides meeting. Attacked, raped and strangled and it seemed that every copper in town was working on the case. But not Percy Copper.

Here was the chance to keep his name to the forefront. But no, he had not been assigned to duty on the case. Here he was, patrolling his beat as usual, as if nothing else was going on, whilst others were making a name for themselves at his expense.

He felt like kicking through a shop window in frustration. He was on night shift again as well, where the only chance of glory was the arrest of a few drunks or the breaking up a half-hearted scuffle as the pubs turned out at 10.30. Percy had complained to Inspector Eddie Trueman, the head of uniform branch, asking to be put on the murder team, but was told brusquely that ordinary policing still had to carry on, beats had to be walked, minor arrests to be made, traffic to be directed, complaints to be investigated, the continuing day-to-day routine that keeps the streets of the town relatively crime-free. 'Can't have everyone glory-seeking, can we, son? Coppering is doing as you're told. We don't always like it, but it goes with the job.'

'But sir, it would be good experience for me.'

'How long have you been in the job, Percy?'

'Since last October, sir, nine, ten months.'

'Thee's still wet behind the ears, lad, nine months? The first nine months I was on the job I never got to even see an inspector, let alone make demands on him. Get thissen out there and do your job. Experience will come along in time right enough. You're keen to get on and I like that but, in the meantime, you've got a beat to patrol.'

'Yessir.'

There was nothing else he could say and so now he paced along his beat. He rattled shop doors to check they were locked, looked into the back yards of premises, shining his torch into all corners and peered through shop windows to check for intruders. Somewhere out there, maybe in this very street, there lurked a child-killer, a murderous, raping bastard, whilst he, Percy Copper, escorted the gin-sodden, piss-stinking Widow Blackburn as she staggered home from the Dog and Duck, making sure that she got home safely and didn't trip over the pavement and break her hip or whatever.

Percy had visions of spotting a suspicious character creeping about after midnight with a small canvas haversack in his hand. As Percy approaches, the man turns and runs. Percy chases after him, bringing him down to the ground with a flying rugby tackle and subdues him. On opening the runner's haversack, he finds Judy Dennison's missing Guides uniform and realises he has singly-handedly caught her killer

PC Percy Copper; the hero of the hour once again.

It was a fantasy played out in his mind as he patrolled down Fenwick Street. On the other side of the road, Percy noticed a woman sitting on a low wall. It was getting late, past closing time, there was a chilly wind and it had been raining; not the night to be out sitting on a wall. As he approached, he realised that she was sobbing into her hands.

'You all right, love?' he asked, shining his torch at her, trying not to shine it in her eyes.

'No, I'm bastard well not. What's it got to do wi' you, anyhow?'

'It's me job, love. Giving a helping hand where we can.'

He was close by her now. She was a small woman, possibly in her early forties, dark hair cut short, round face, her eyes red from weeping, wearing a flower-patterned dress and red cardigan, but no coat. She twisted her wedding ring round and round and round about her ring finger. He squatted down onto his haunches beside her.

'Well, you can take your helping hand and piss off. It's nowt to do with you and there's sod all you can do to help.'

'You don't know until you ask, do you?'

'All right then, tell us where he is, the bastard.'

'Who are we talking about, love?'

'Next door's cat, of course. What do you think? Me bastard husband, that's who.'

'Oh, right. He's gone missing and you're worried about him, like?'

'Yeah, worried I'll cut his lying, cheating heart out if I ever find him, more like.'

'Oh!' answered Percy, suddenly unsure how to proceed. He had not had to deal with a domestic incident before.

'Yeah, "oh"! That about says it all, don't it? Like I said, less'n you know where he is, or where *she* lives, the bitch, you're no sodding use and you might as well bugger off.'

'Look, love, it's cold and wet, s'not a night to be out like this, is it? You'll catch your death.'

'And who'd give a shit, eh? Not that bastard, that's for sure!' She spat vehemently.

'How... how do you know, like, he's gone... astray?'

She gave him that look, the sort of look you give to dogs and idiots. 'It's Tuesday, right? Tuesday night is his bowls night. Every Tuesday, without fail, he goes to the club, plays while it's still light and then has a beer or two at the club bar. Maybe a game of darts, right?'

'Yeah, if you say so.'

'So how can he play bowls without his bowls, eh? He didn't take his bowls wi' him. I went to put the broom away in the cupboard under the stairs and there they were, his bowls. So, what's he up to? Playing around with Debbie Merchant that works with him, that's what and the bitch lives here, on Fenwick Street somewhere. And when I find 'em, I'll likely strangle one of 'em. Hey, not literally you twonk,' she exclaimed, seeing the look on Percy's face. 'Maybe scratch her eyes out, though. Rip her nipples off.'

'Don't do nothing stupid, will you? What's your name by the way? I should've asked you earlier.'

'Janice. Janice Johnson. My lying, cheating, no good, ever-loving bastard of a husband is Dave Johnson.'

'And where's home, Janice?'

'Ranmoor Street. Number 22.'

'Ranmoor Street? That's in...'

'Aye, Marpleside, bloody miles away, I know.' Janice Johnson shook her head resignedly and slowly got to her feet, brushing the dirt and moss from the seat of her skirt with her hand, wrapping her arms about herself as if suddenly realising that she was feeling cold. 'I'm not doing any good here, am I?'

'No, Janice, not really.'

'You're prob'ly right' she sighed. 'I'm just making an exhibition of myself, aren't I? I mean, I could sit here all night, couldn't I and still not find 'em.'

'That's right, no guarantee at all you'll find them, they mightn't even be here. You don't know for sure that, er, Dave is even with this woman.'

'Oh, I know all right. A wife knows these things. She might be the last to know but once she knows, she knows... if that makes any bloody sense?'

'Yeah, sure, not bein' a wife myself I can't rightly say.' He looked at her again. Her cardigan was wet, the back of her dress was wet where she had been sitting and her damp hair was stuck to the side of her face. 'You know, you really need to get on home and out of them wet clothes, I meant it about catching your death. It's no night to be out without a coat.'

'Aye, you're right, but it's just I were so mad, I just rushed out of the house without thinking.' She stood there, looking up and down the street for one last time, as if expecting her husband to suddenly reveal himself. 'Off you go then,' she said to Percy, not looking at him. 'And thanks.'

'You sure you're OK?' Percy asked, reluctant to leave her. 'You're not going to do... anything stupid, are you?' he asked once more.

'No, I'm not going to go and jump off Redemption Bridge if that's what you're thinking.'

'No', he answered hurriedly, 'of course not,' but that was exactly what had crossed his mind.

'Look, I'm doing meself no good here, I can see that. I've got time to catch the last bus home and I'll have it out with Dave when he gets home. If he ever does. If not, well, I'll cross that particular bridge that when I get to it.' Janice wiped her eyes on a tiny square of embroidered handkerchief, straightened herself up, took a deep breath and started to walk away. She turned back. 'Thanks for the shoulder, I'm fine now, honest.'

'I'll walk down with you, see you're OK.'

'Making sure I don't jump off Redemption eh?' she responded, with a faint glimmer of a smile.

'No, it's not that, but I can walk you down as far as Sheffield Road, it's on my beat, see, and then it's only a hop and step across the road and down Blonk Street to t' bus station. What time's the last one to Marpleside anyhow?'

'11.25, twenty-five past.'

Percy consulted his watch: 11.12. 'We'd best get a move on, then. You'd not want to miss that. You got your bus fare?' he asked as an afterthought.

'Yes, yes thanks,' she answered, showing him her handbag.

Percy then escorted her as far as Sheffield Road. 'There you go, love, take care now.'

'And you. And thanks. You know, I never did get to know your name?'

'Percy, Percy Copper, PC 4126. Any problems, just ask for me at the desk in the nick. Percy Copper...'

'I will do, and thanks, Percy,' she said, wrapping her arms again about her shivering body, the red cardigan offering little protection against the biting wind.

He watched her cross the street by the zebra crossing, the Belisha beacon shining out brightly orange in the gloom of the night. A scurry of wind sent a sheet of ragged newspaper hurrying on after her. He made a note in his pocketbook, just in case the body of a David Johnson should turn up or a Debbie Merchant had her nipples ripped off.

His beat continued down towards the West Riding Bank where he had lost his fingertip in the foiled bank robbery, past an estate agent's window displaying a nice cottage in Fenmoor village that he wanted but could not afford. He walked on past Redmires department store then turned up Glassmaker Street; not that there had ever been a glassmaker in the town so far as anyone could determine, just as no one had ever found paradise in Paradise Square.

He was near the end of his second turn around his beat and he found, much to his surprise, that he felt a sense of satisfaction at the thought that, in a small way, his action had been probably just as important as finding the killer of Judy Devonshire.

# AS SURE AS EGGS ARE EGGS
## THE WESTERN FRONT, FRANCE. 1916

Shyly, Jeanette handed over the crumpled brown paper bag, inside which were six eggs, five white and one brown. Private Arthur Pink mumbled his thanks, shuffling his feet, barely able to look the girl in the face. He was pleased with the gift; fresh eggs were unheard of so close to the front line and he was sure the rest of his platoon would be delighted; they might stop ribbing him if he brought such a welcome gift.

'Aye, thanks again,' he muttered and began to shuffle away from her, desperately confused and embarrassed.

Jeanette was the daughter of the owner of the local *estimanet*, the bar and café frequented by all the troops in reserve, at rest from the front line. She was the object of admiration of all the soldiers, could have her pick of any of them, so quite why she had been so taken with the shy, awkward, mumbling Arthur she could never say. Perhaps it was a burgeoning mothering instinct, perhaps she just felt sorry for him as he seemed to be the object of endless practical jokes, but whatever the reason, of all the hundreds of troops who passed through the bar, Arthur was the one who had caught her eye.

She stood there expectantly, face upraised, wanting him to kiss her. She could not tell him that, but surely he must realise? Arthur wanted to kiss her but did not know how. He blushed to the roots at the very thought of it. The only female he had ever kissed was his mother, when he kissed her on the cheek as he said goodbye.

'Aye, right, well, best be off I s'pose,' he mumbled again.

Jeanette's command of English was not very extensive, but she could readily understand that her overtures were not being reciprocated and her tender feelings towards Arthur began to evaporate and she felt like snatching the precious eggs back from him. With a theatrical 'harrumph' of injured pride, Jeanette turned on her heels and walked away.

Arthur, realising that somehow he had offended her, called half-heartedly after her, but she took no notice. With a sigh and a shrug of resignation, Arthur, too, turned away and began to head back towards the barn where his troop was billeted.

He could hear the sound of heavy artillery from the front lines, but gunfire was so common as to go unnoticed; Arthur was already thinking how best to cook the eggs. They could be fried, but the only thing to fry them with was the rancid butter that came in a tin. Not good. Boiling would be alright, except it would be hard to share six boiled eggs between eleven men. Scrambled would be best, he thought, and easy to divide; go down a treat that would. Mind, they would be better with a slice of Dad's crusty white bloomer, fresh from the oven with a knob of best butter. Still musing, Arthur walked on, not realising the he was being followed.

Sitting by the front window of the bar, Sergeant-Major Hargreaves had watched the interplay between Jeanette and Arthur, sourly amused at Pink's pathetic failure with the girl. *If it had been me*, he thought, *I'd'ave had her round the back of the bar in no time*. He drained his glass of plonk – vin blanc – not as good as a pint of good English ale but it did the trick and he set out after Arthur.

'What you got there, lad?' Hargreaves demanded as he came

up behind Arthur. Arthur was so surprised, he almost dropped the bag of eggs.

'Er... nothing, nothing, Sergeant-Major.'

'Looks like contraband to me, I've had my eye on you, Pink. Consorting with the enemy is a serious offence, court-martial job.'

Arthur, not the sharpest bayonet in the British Army, was confused. Jeanette was French, so how could she be the enemy? And he hadn't consorted with her, just been given some eggs, that's all.

'No, Sergeant-Major, just some eggs, is all, share with the lads, like.'

'Eggs! Eggs is contraband, son. Eggs is banned, eggs is.' Hargreaves leaned in closer, his face inches away from Arthur. 'Why do you think eggs is banned, eh? So close to the German line?' Arthur shook his head in bemused perplexity. ''Cos the Germans poison the chickens, that's why, makes 'em lay poisoned eggs.'

'Poisoned?'

'Aye lad, terrible poison, rots your gizzards like acid and you was going to let your mates eat them. That's attempted murder, lad.'

'No, honest, I didn't know.'

'Best give 'em to me, eh?' Hargreaves said sympathetically. 'I'll cover your tracks and if you says nowt, none'll be the wiser. Pass 'em over, lad, and I'll see them destroyed proper, like. Don't want the poison to escape, do we now?'

'No. No, Sergeant.'

'And you keep away from that lass at the bar, she's a German secret agent and the Redcaps have got their eyes on her. You don't want to be caught up in that, do you, lad? Could be nasty if they think you're part of the plot. That's a firing squad job.'

'No, Sergeant,' Arthur said, swallowing hard, handing over the bag of eggs as if it was on fire.

Hargreaves sniggered cruelly to himself as he watched

Arthur hurry away. Now what to do with the eggs? Hargreaves had no intention of sharing them with the Sergeants' Mess, but he'd see Sergant Binks, the company cook; Binks would take a couple of eggs for himself but that was OK. Hargreaves would still have four eggs left. He would scrounge a rasher or two of streaky bacon and fry them with that.

Still smiling to himself, Hargreaves set off to find Binks.

In his observation post in the shell-pocked church tower, Captain Miller laid down his binoculars. He had been studying the German trench lines but there'd been no activity and, bored and restless, he'd begun to look around elsewhere. He had also witnessed Arthur and Jeanette, seen the package change hands and then seen Hargreaves intercept Pink and relieve him of the paper bag. His curiosity roused, Captain Miller descended from the tower and, in turn, intercepted Hargreaves and the precious package of eggs.

'Sergeant-Major,' he called. 'Show me the package you took from that soldier.'

'Package, sir?'

'Yes, Hargreaves, the package in your hand that you took from Private Pink.'

'Oh that. Just something e' borrowed, sir. He was returning it, that's all.'

'I saw the girl give it to him, Hargreaves, don't give me the lie.'

'No sir.'

'So?'

'Contraband, sir, confiscated it,' Hargreaves, muttered, barely civil. Miller thought Hargreaves to be a bully and tyrant, the worst kind of Sergeant-Major and was sure that whatever was in the bag, Hargreaves had taken it for his own use.

'Bring it here.' Reluctantly, Hargreaves passed over the bag. 'Eggs?' Miller said, on opening the bag. 'Hardly contraband.'

'Pink, he… he wanted me to 'ave 'em, appreciation, like, for helping 'im.'

'I don't think so. Thieving from your men is a serious offence. It could cost you your stripes – and more.'

Hargreaves seethed inside but there was little he could do. 'Just a joke, sir, I was going to let him have them back,'

'Let me do that, Sergeant-Major. Save you the trouble.'

Captain Miller had every intention of returning the eggs, but it was so long since he had had a fresh egg that the intention soon fell away. After all, he reasoned, Private Pink was already resigned to their loss and would be none the wiser. Miller hurried off to his billet and called for Jenkins, his batman.

'Some eggs, Jenkins. I'll have two in an omelette with my supper, keep the rest safe and I'll have two boiled for breakfast.'

'Very good, sir.'

*It's all right for some,* thought Jenkins, *he could've at least given me one,* trying to remember when last he's had a fresh egg. Then he had a thought. If he took two eggs out for himself and hid them, he could 'accidentally' drop the bag and say all the eggs were broken. He could boil the others once the coast was clear. They'd be nice with a cup of the captain's special tea.

'Terrible sorry, sir, he said later on, full of contrition, ''fraid I dropped the bag of eggs. All smashed, they is.'

'Show me,' said Miller, tight-lipped with anger. 'How could you be so clumsy?'

'I just came over all faint, sir, and me 'ands had no strength.'

'I'll give you faint!' Miller snapped. He inspected the soggy bag. Yellow strings of yoke leaked through the paper and crushed shells crunched under his fingers as he turned the bag over. Suspicious, he ripped the bag open and counted the broken shells; even though they were severely crushed, it was still possible to count them. Four! Only four eggshells! He looked at Jenkins' guilt-ridden face.

'It seems to me, Jenkins, that possibly you put two eggs aside for my omelette and forgot about them. Is that correct?'

'Oh, yes sir, 'course, now I remembers. Getting terrible, my memory is.'

'If it fails you again, you'll be in very hot water.'

'Just like them eggs was going to be tomorrow, eh?' Jenkins said, in feeble humour.

Jenkins 'found' the 'misplaced' eggs, one brown and one white. He broke the white egg into the bowl and then broke the brown, ready to be whisked up for the Captain's omelette

The pungent, sulphurous stench of rotten egg pervaded the tiny kitchen of Captain Miller's billet.

It seemed as though nobody was going to enjoy an egg that day.

# PORTENTS

## THE PRESENT DAY. WHENEVER THAT IS.

We need some explanations and background here. Some context. Context! Described in the Oxford Dictionary of the English Language as: *noun; the circumstances that form the setting for an event, statement or idea, and in terms of which it can be clearly understood.*

Now, I never much liked history at school. Why learn about things which happened hundreds of years ago? Apart from the battles and bloody bits, that is and there are plenty of battles and bloody bits to come, but in order to understand this account, the context of this story, there has to be a history lesson.

Besides, as Alan Bennett would have it, 'history is just one fucking thing after another'. So here we go, just one fucking thing after another.

India, the fabled lands of India, the Jewel in the Crown of Empire. We need to go to June 23$^{rd}$, 1757, and the Battle of Plassey.

Plassey, some 150 km north of Calcutta where the armies of the British East India Company under Robert Clive, Clive of India, defeated Siraj-ud-daulah, the Nawab of Bengal (of the Black Hole of Calcutta infamy) and his French allies. The decisive victory that secured British interests in India and kicked out the French for good. *Au revoir, mes amis* and good riddance.

OK, I know that that's a totally simplistic point of view, but it is essentially correct, and it is not germane to this story to go into the duplicity and double-dealing that went on behind the scenes leading up to the battle, the subsequent flight of Siraj-ud-daulah from the battle with his favourite wives and most valuable jewellery and then his betrayal and murder. He was supplanted as Nawab of Bengal by Mir Jahir, a ruler more acceptable to the Honourable East India Company (although he was ousted in his turn when he proved less compliant than the British considered necessary).

It is called diplomacy.

Now, imagine if you will the battlefield after Plassey. Picture yourself amidst the carnage of the battlefield, amongst the dead and dying, the screams of the wounded, the puddles of blood and heaps of viscera and blasted limbs, the acrid reek of gunpowder and the smoke from countless funeral fires, smashed field guns, discarded weapons, unmindful of the exhausted soldiers wandering the artillery-shredded landscape, ignoring the squads of local women stripping and looting the dead, the countless eviscerated cavalry and pack horses, a dozen or so dismembered elephants torn apart by howitzer and field guns and the frenzied attentions of scavenging vultures, kites, cranes, magpies and crows, so bloated with the abundant human flesh that they can barely hop from one corpse to another.

Amidst all this death and blood and mayhem sits a sadhu, a holy man. He is naked, having cast aside his saffron robe and loincloth. His hair is long and matted into thick, rope-like dread-locks called Jata, his body daubed with white powder made from dried cow dung, and the three horizontal stripes across his forehead, his tilaka, denote his devotion to Shiva the Destroyer.

Light rain spatters his body, pearlescent beads sprinkle his face and beard and rainwater runnels carve their way through the white cow-dung coating on his body. His eyes are wide open,

47

fixed and staring at nothing and you would be surprised to see that they are of a startlingly bright blue. In deep meditation, he sits in the lotus position, his hands resting lightly on his knees with his thumb pressing into his first and second fingers, his breathing deep and heavy, his head thrown back in ecstasy as the charrus (marijuana) induced vision surges into his being.

He sees blood and lightning, hears the thunder of the gods as they drive the unbelievers into the sea, the pale-skinned destroyers of caste, of belief, the red-faced devils from across the seas; in exactly one hundred years the people will rise, the Angreji will be defeated and destroyed, a new Hindu Emperor will sit upon the throne and the divine order as ordained by the gods will be restored. All this he can see, all this he knows, all this is foretold, all this is inevitable, all this is the divine prophesy as issued by the almighty Shiva, the Destroyer; all this is the inexorable death of the defilers, the usurpers, the end of the British rule in India.

It is written, the gods have spoken. The gods have spoken and Janaki Gipi Mhairi, the mystic naga sadhu, is the chosen messenger of the gods. So be it. It is written in the fires of the battlefield and will come to pass in 1857.

Is that how it happened? How the 100 year prediction came into being? A naked sadhu sitting in a blood-soaked battlefield receiving the prophecy in a marijuana-vision? I don't know, but it is a darned sight more interesting than to simply say that in 1757 there was a prophecy which said that in a hundred years' time, the British will be driven from India.

However it came about at that particular time, there is no doubt that the Plassey prophecy assumed a mythical significance for many Hindus as the beginning of the historical cycle preordained in ancient obscure Hindu writings, which foretold the fall of the Muslim Moghul Raj, the rule of foreign invaders which would last exactly one hundred years and then the rise of a new powerful Hindu Raj. It is written and scheduled to come to pass in 1857 and agitators spread the word accordingly.

It is written.

In 1857, one hundred years after Plassey, the garrison at Meerut rose up in arms and the Indian Mutiny erupted across northern India, spreading death and destruction.

*Oh, come and look*
*In the bazaar of Meerut*
*The Feringi is waylaid and beaten.*
*The white man is waylaid and beaten*
*In the open bazaar of Meerut*
*Look! Oh look!*


It was written.

# THE WINDTOWER EFFECT
## THE PRESENT DAY. WHENEVER THAT IS.

'I'm telling you, Paul, Windtower can't lose, trust me on this.'

'Windtower? No, he's got no form at that distance. He might go for a place if he's lucky, but never a win, not with the quality of field that's running in that race.'

'Trust me, Paul, I'm telling you for a fact, a one hundred percent certain fact, that Windtower is going to win the 3.30 on Saturday. Guaranteed!'

'You mean there's a fix in?'

'I'm not going to confirm a thing like that now, am I?' Gerry put his arm about me in a friendly, conspiratorial manner. 'But there again, I'm not going to deny it, either.'

Gerry was my friend, a reasonably successful jockey, never going to hit the big time, but always in work. He and his wife Maggie had been neighbours of ours; chats over the garden fence, drinks at Christmas, that sort of thing, but never close. However, when my wife Brenda left me for an insurance salesman, I was totally devastated, and Gerry and Maggie had rallied round to help me get over it and became true friends

To take me out of myself one day, Gerry took me to the races, to Newmarket where he was riding, and I have been hooked ever since.

Hooked in a big way. Those who say that gambling is not an addiction do not know what they are talking about. I lived for gambling. I, who had never known which end of a horse was which, now studied the form book with a dedication for study I had never shown at school or university. I could tell you the form of every horse on the card, their sire and dam, number of races, where they raced, wins and places, horses raced against, weights carried, distances run, jockeys ridden, the going soft or firm – and how much money I had won or lost on every horse I had ever backed.

At first, it was only on-course betting when I accompanied Gerry to his rides. (Brenda and I had set up a successful on-line real estate company but after the divorce, I had sold the business for a healthy profit and even after handing over Brenda's share, I still had time and money to spare whilst I decided what to do next.)

I wrote my own racing form analysis program, hours spent on my computer feeding in all possible computations of form; horses, weather, courses, jockeys, weights, distances, opposition etc, looking for patterns to identify the long-shot, the high odds non-favourite that brings in the big wins.

And it worked; not every time, of course, but often enough so that over a period, the wins outweighed the inevitable losses. I then opened a credit betting account with Cuthbert Pye (known as Custard Pye but never to his face), who ran a number of local betting shops. My credit rating was good, I paid up on my losses on time and my system seemed to be working.

And then it wasn't working quite so well. Nothing drastic, simply that the interval between the big wins and the losses got imperceptibly longer. The money from the sale of the business dwindled.

Custard Pye extended my credit. I tweaked the program, which helped for a while and so I placed bigger and bigger bets to cover what I owed to Pye. And the losses mounted up. My debts got bigger.

I took out a loan against my house – I'd paid Brenda for her share of the house out of the proceeds from the sale of the business – and that kept Custard Pye at bay for a while.

I spent longer and longer on my PC and with the form book, covering every aspect of every horse I was backing, avidly reading every racing columnist for tips.

I had some big wins. And I had some substantial losses.

Custard Pye kindly extended my credit again. Gerry and Maggie were getting concerned. The racing world is a small world and the extent of my gambling – and the extent of my losses – could not be kept a secret.

'You've got to get a grip there,' Gerry cautioned. 'Custard Pye is nice as pie to your face, but he's a hard villain when he's looking for payment. He's got these bruisers from Newcastle, Sealskin and Boiler if you could ever believe such names, debt collectors they call themselves, but they're just hired muscle, leg-breakers.'

I reassured him it was under control. Which, of course, it wasn't, but he seemed satisfied.

I placed some more bets and lost some more money. Then I had a 'friendly' visit from the Newcastle heavies; not that they laid a finger on me, but the threat was there right enough.

Jelly Doughnut was the horse to put everything right. I ran the system through more than a dozen times and every time it came up with Jelly Doughnut as the winner at long odds: at least 14 to 1

I owed Custard Pye £32,000. I owed some other bookies as well, but Sealskin and Boiler had made it known that customer loyalty was expected from me and that all my bets had to be placed with Pye. I put £10,000 on Jelly Doughnut. A win at better than 10 to 1 would clear all my debts with the bookies, repay the bank loans and still have some left over as the ante for future bets.

The wretched beast fell at the first fence.

I was seriously in trouble now and that is when I told Gerry and Maggie just how serious my plight was. Gerry said nothing for a while and then said, 'Let me think about it for a bit. In this business there's always a way, if you just go about it in the right manner.'

Sealskin and Boiler paid another visit, not quite so friendly this time, asking me how good the local hospital was, did I know a good orthopaedic surgeon, encouraging stuff like that.

It was about two weeks later that Gerry told me that his ride, Windtower, was 'guaranteed' to win the 3.30 at Cheltenham. I ran the system. A good horse but no finishing speed, unlikely to compete with the strong field declared for the race. A place would be the best I could expect, and I never made place bets. Also, the odds would probably be no better than 9 to1.

'Trust me, Paul, I'm telling you for a fact, a one hundred percent certain fact, that Windtower is going to win the 3.30 on Saturday. Guaranteed.'

He was a good jockey and a good friend. If there was a fix in so that Gerry could 'guarantee' the win on Windtower, it could be the solution to all my problems. 'Trust me,' he said again, 'put everything you can raise on Windtower and after you've got straight, promise me you'll seek help. Gamblers Anonymous, OK? And Paul, this is a one-time thing, can only be done the once.'

I did just that, borrowed on the house again, using up all the equity, but once Windtower came home I would be clear and straight, Custard Pye would be out of my life and Gamblers Anonymous would have a new member. Maybe.

It was 3.30 on race day. They're off! Broken Biscuits led from Mousetrap, followed by Bluebird Horizons, the favourite. Windtower was tucked in about 7th or 8th. The first fence was cleared easily, no horses down. My heart was beating so wildly I thought it would burst out of my rib cage. The second fence and one of the back markers went down. Windtower was now up to 6th and Gerry in the purple and gold colours of the Arab owner was easily identifiable. They cleared the next five fences without incident, with no real positional changes. At the next fence, Broken Biscuits went down heavily and Windtower had to swerve suddenly avoid him. My heart was in my mouth, I could scarcely breathe.

Windtower moved smoothly up to 4th, tucked in behind Bluebird Horizons in 3rd, Mousetrap leading but fading fast. Barnaby's Cat, Bluebird Horizons and Windtower easily swept past Mousetrap as they ran up to the next fences, all horses safely over. A gap opened up between the leading three horses and the chasing pack.

At the next, Barnaby's Cat mistimed his jump and Bluebird Horizons and Windtower overtook him as he went down.

Three fences to go!

I did not think I could stand the strain; my shirt was soaked through with nervous perspiration even though it was a cold, blustery day. The next fence was safely cleared. Two fences to go and Windtower was now neck and neck with Bluebird Horizons as they raced up to the penultimate fence. And Bluebird Horizons got it all wrong, tangled his hind legs and nearly went down but Windtower was clear and in the lead. 'Come on, come on, come on!' I shouted, hoarse with excitement. Once over the final fence Windtower was clear and home and I was saved.

Then disaster struck. Just as they came up to the fence, Gerry's foot slipped out of the stirrup, his weight was unbalanced and Windtower, without the jockey's signal, missed his jumping point and tangled heavily into the fence, nearly unseating Gerry. *Nooooooo*!!!!. They somehow scrambled over the fence, with Gerry hanging on for dear life as they raced for the finish line. But Bluebird Horizons was close behind, closing fast and Windtower's lack of finishing speed did for him. Bluebird Horizons beat him easily by two lengths. And I was ruined.

I waited for Gerry in the car park, for we had travelled up together as usual.

He was all smiles. I could not believe it. He was laughing at me.

'So how does it feel, lover boy?' he asked. 'After all we did, how could you? How could you have done that to me? How could you have slept with Maggie?'

And I knew then that he could have won – that he had lost deliberately. Still laughing, he got in the car and drove off, just as Sealskin and Boiler started to make their way over to me.

# SHADOWS OF A DREAM
## NORTH EAST ENGLAND. JUNE 1914

'How do, Isaac,' Molly Hindle said, coming up behind him as he walked down Whitton Lane towards Adlard's forge. 'Where're you off to, then?'

'Nowhere really, just down to t'forge,' Isaac Garforth answered, his head jerking back and forth as he looked around to make sure that no one could see him talking to a girl, especially his twin brother Saul. 'Where's thee going to?'

'Me Mam sent us out t'house, me Auntie Myrtle's come round, and she's got some problem with me Uncle Albert and me Mam didn't want me to hear what's being said.'

'Oh aye, what's the problem then?' he asked, although Isaac, just a few weeks past his fourteenth birthday, was not in the least bit interested. He was far more concerned with getting away from the highly public Whitton Lane, where just about the entire village could see him with Molly Hindle.

'Don't know really, except me Auntie Myrtle's crying and I heard Mam say, "Well I never, the dirty beast", or summat like that, then she saw me listening on the stairs and sent me out. Anyhow, what's thee going down to t'forge for? Getting yourself some new shoes?' Molly asked.

'New shoes? Oh aye, dead funny, I don't think.'

'So, what're you going for then?'

'Nowt, really, I just like to go and watch.'

'Can I come with thee? I've got nowt else to do,' she asked and fell into step alongside him, giving him a big smile as she did so.

'Well, you'd prob'ly find it right boring.'

'I don't mind, Isaac. Not so long as I'm with you,' and she briefly laid her hand on his arm, causing him to blush to his roots. He liked Molly a lot, but he dreaded the prospect of being seen with her; he would never live it down if his twin brother Saul saw them together. He pulled down his flat cap low over his eyes and hunched his head down into his shoulders in the hope that he wouldn't be recognised if anybody saw him with Molly.

Off to the left, the blackened brick of the engine house and heapstead buildings of the mine-workings towered over the narrow streets of the pit village like a fortress on a hill. The high summer sun glinted and shivered through the spinning spokes of the headstock pulley wheel, sending shattered shards of bright orange sunlight to harden and coalesce the shadows of the doorways and alleyways along the street. Isaac could visualize Saul hiding in the deep shade, lurking like a pike in the reeds, waiting to leap out, ready to mock and ridicule him.

They walked further on down the road, Isaac still hunched down, hoping to be invisible, when Molly suddenly clutched his arm. 'Ooh, look, is that your Saul over there?'

'*What*? *Where*? *WHERE*?' Isaac looked around wildly.

'Oh no, sorry, it weren't, must be someone else,' Molly said, all innocence, gazing at some distant nothing, her eyes sparkling, finding it hard not to burst out laughing.

'You did that on bloody purpose!' Isaac shouted angrily.

'You shouldn't swear. My Mam says that people what swear only go to prove how ignorant they are. Lacking in vocabu... vocable-berry. Goes to show they don't know many words.'

'Near on freet me to death.'

'Are you that frightened of Saul, then?'

'Nah, gerraway. It's just... well, tha knows. Being with a girl and all, he'll think I'm soft.'

'I don't think it's soft to be seen with a girl, Isaac.'

'Well, that's 'cos thee's a lass, that's why. Lasses know nowt.'

As they came up on the forge, Isaac could hear the dull pounding of hammers on the anvil and his pulses quickened, racing to the beating cadence of forged iron. He loved the smithy, loved the smells of the red and yellow glowing coke and of the dull, red-hot metal and the sweaty steam of horses waiting to be shod. Isaac spent hours just watching, peering through the open window, mesmerised by the showers of incandescent sparks cascading like roman candles from the beaten yellow-hot iron, listening to the crash of hammers and the dragon's-breath hiss of the bellows heating up the furnace, drawing in the sights and sounds and smells; wishing that he, too, could become a black-smith. Isaac wished that more than anything in the world but knew it would never happen; it was like wishing for the stars.

His father had told him, many times, that as soon as he and Saul were fourteen, they were to leave school and follow him down the mine, as had generations of Garforth men before him. The prospect of going down the mine appalled Isaac. He dreaded it with a fear that woke him up in a sweat and he yearned for the forge, ached for a chance to become a black-smith, but his father had spoken, and Jack Garforth's word was law. Isaac could no more speak out against his father's wishes than he could cut off his own arm.

'What do you come down here for then, Isaac?' Molly asked

'Just like it. That's all. Just like it.' He bridled defensively. 'Nowt wrong wi' that, is there?'

'Never said there was, did I? Just curious why you want to come here?'

'I told thee,' Isaac growled, 'I just like it,' and immediately felt sorry for having spoken so sharply. 'Well, actually Molly, I'd like to be a blacksmith, working with iron and that. Making shoes for the horses. Repairing ploughshares and the like. Far rather be doing that than going down t'pit.' He looked at Molly to see if she were laughing at him; he had never told a living soul about his secret ambitions before.

'So why don't you?'

'Because me Dad, he's said I'm to go down t'pit. And then there's the apprenticeship costs. Two bob a week or more it'd cost and me dad'll not pay anything like that. That's why.'

''Ave you asked?'

'Nay. No point, is there? 'E's set his mind on Saul and me going down pit and thee knows my dad, once he makes up his mind, nowt'll shift it, not even black powder. He says it'll keep us in order, but I wouldn't need keeping in order if I were doing what I wanted, would I? I mean, I only cause trouble in school 'cos they try to make me do something I can't do.'

'Like what? What do they make you do that you can't? You could do anything you wanted, Isaac. Honest.'

'I mean, it's like with the writing, aint'it? 'Cos I'm cack-handed. They won't let me use my left hand, and they force me to try and use my right hand. When I were little, they even tied my hand, my left hand, up behind my back. To make me use my right. Well, I couldn't. Not properly. So, all my writing were all wrong.'

'I remember that, in Mrs Spurling's class? It's cruel. Right cruel. It's not your fault, is it?'

'Mrs Spurling said I were sinister. Always remember that. Sinister! And if I ever used my left hand, often as not without even thinking, she used to hit it, dead hard. Said it was the devil's mark. I suppose that's why I got to be a big nuisance in class. Couldn't do the work 'cos I couldn't write proper, so...' Isaac shrugged eloquently. 'So that's why Saul and me always made a nuisance of us'self.'

'But what 'bout Saul? He's not left-handed.'

'Nay. He's just a varmint, a right little bugger, as my Dad says.'

Molly looked earnestly at Isaac. 'You really do want to be a blacksmith, don't you, Isaac? You want it really bad; I can see it in your eyes.'

'Aye,' he sighed, 'but wanting it and doing it are two different things.'

'Honestly, Isaac,' she said, pleading with her eyes, 'you can do anything you want, you just have to set your mind to it. *Anything*. You can fly as high as the birds if that's what you want, but you've got to do it for yourself.'

'There's no point, I tell thee.'

'How do you know? You don't, not until you ask.'

'There's the cost of the apprenticeship. Me dad'll not wear that.'

'So? How much is the apprenticeship?'

'Don't know exactly. Two, three, four bob a week.'

'So? Go and find out. Go on, get yourself in there right now and ask Mr Adlard.'

'He'll say no, bugger off.'

'You don't know, do you? And even if he does say... that, what've you lost, eh? Nowt!'

''He'll still not take me. Because of being left-handed. I couldn't work in there, hammering with me right hand. I'd take somebody's fingers off.'

'You don't know any such thing, not unless thee asks.'

'Why aye, I suppose thee's right.'

'Get on in then.'

'Aye, right,' Isaac said, without much conviction, shuffling his feet around in the dirt, not wanting to look her in the eye.

'Go on then.'

'Aye, right,' Isaac said, but made no effort to move.

'You want me to hold your hand and go in with thee?'

'Nay! Get off, don't be so daft.'

'Get on in, then.'

'Aye, right.' And Isaac took a deep breath. 'Fly as high as the birds, you said?' He squared his shoulders, straightened his flat cap, gave Molly a nervous grin and walked on in to the side door of the forge.

'Dad?' Isaac asked apprehensively, his nervousness so great that it clogged his throat. His stomach was so twisted up in knots that he felt sick, his heart beat furiously and he could only breathe in shallow pants. Ever since he had returned from the forge, he had been trying to find an opportunity to talk to his father, but the right moment never seemed to come. And, if the truth be known, he was afraid of his dad and he felt, deep inside, that there would never be a right moment to speak out against his wishes.

'Aye, lad?' Jack Garforth answered, as he laid down his newspaper and picked up his pipe.

'I were down at t'forge today, this after – you know, Mr Adlard's? – an' he said he can take me on as an apprentice, for only two bob a week, that's all, as I'm dead keen and been going down for ages and I'd really like to do that, Dad, really, all my life I reckon, been wanting to do that. So, can I, Dad? Please?' Isaac made his speech without drawing breath so that the words came out in a garbled verbal avalanche, gushing so quickly, it was hard to tell where one word finished and another took up.

'Hold on, son. Not so fast. Calm yourself down and take it a bit at a time.'

'Aye, right.' Isaac's initial nervousness had gone now, the die was cast. He took a deep breath and then spoke distinctly and slowly. 'I were saying, Dad, I went to see Mr Adlard, this after… this afternoon… you know Mr Adlard down at the forge?'

'Aye, I know Henry Adlard, right enough.'

'I were asking him about an apprenticeship. To work with him at the forge.'

When Mary Garforth, his mother, heard Isaac say this, she

closed her eyes as she felt a huge surge of relief. 'Thank the Lord' she whispered to herself, her prayers answered, 'he's not to go down the pit.'

Mary's first husband and elder brother had both died underground and the thought of Isaac and Saul going down the mine had filled her with a dread that clogged up her heart. The pit was always hungry for men, insatiable; it devoured men with a ferocity that was almost satanic, taking man and boy alike and no mother could ever feel sanguine about her children going down the mine.

As she wiped a trickled tear of relief away from her cheek, she heard Jack ask of Isaac, 'And you want to be bound apprentice to him, is that right?' his tone brusque, although not unkindly.

'Aye, Dad, I think that's what I've always wanted to do. I mean, I've spent hours, hours and hours down there at the forge, sometimes talking with Mr Adlard when he's not busy. He knows I'm right keen,'

'And he says he'll take thee on. Without talking to me about it?' A hard edge crept into Jack's voice.

'No, no, Dad, 'course not, he said I've got to talk it over with thee first, and if you agree, to talk with him.'

'I reckon this needs some thinking about. I've already told Mr Baker at the pit that thee and Saul will be starting on as soon as he wants. Be any day now.'

'I know, Dad, I should've said summat earlier, I know, but...' He shrugged, unable to actually say that he was afraid of his father and that it was only the prodding by Molly Hindle that had given him the courage to raise the question of an apprenticeship.

'I think it's a right good idea,' Mary said. She knew her husband was not a cruel man and would not force Isaac down the mines unless there were no option, but he was so terribly stubborn once his mind was made up and so she had to make sure that this alternative was well and truly opened up.

'Maybe so, Mary,' Jack replied, 'but like I say, it needs some thinking on.'

'I never knew you liked the forge, Isaac. How come you never said owt before now?' asked Mary.

'I don't rightly know. I suppose because it were always assumed, right from the start, that me and Saul were going down t'pit and I never thought there were an option else. And then when I spoke to Mr Adlard, and he said he could take me on as apprentice for two shilling...' and he tailed away as Jack held up a hand to interrupt him.

'Before we gets to talking about the money of the thing, Isaac, that's the least on it. What I want to hear from you, son, is how you feel about blacksmithing. Why? Why is it so important for you to be doing this?'

'I can't put it dead right, Dad. All can I say is that inside, inside, it's summat I want to do right badly.'

'What is it about it that you like, Isaac?' Mary asked gently, sensing that Jack had already decided to go along with the boy's wishes. There was a relaxed, contemplative set to Jack's head and body, and she could sense no aura of conflict in him, usually a sure indicator of his mood.

'Best way I can say it, Mam, is to tell you about summat that Mr Adlard told me once and I never forgot it. He said as how they had found some Roman nails up by Hadrian's Wall – thee knows the Roman wall up past Hexham?'

'Aye, lad, I've heard of Hadrian's Wall afore now,' Jack answered dryly.

Isaac took another deep breath, and then carried on. 'They found these nails, see? Big ones,' and he spread his hand wide to indicate size. 'Roman nails. Up by the wall, all bright and shiny and Mr Adlard said they got to be hundreds of years old, but they were all bright and shiny, just as if they'd been hammered out yesterday and I asked him how come they weren't all rusted away and he said it was because they weren't made from steel but from lowmore iron that had been smelted from the iron ore with charcoal, not with coke like they use nowadays. And he said summat else, Mr Adlard, summat else that really stopped me, made me think. He said as how the same type of nails would have been used for Jesus' crucifixion, when they nailed him up on the cross.'

'Good Heavens above! Just think on that, Jack. The same nails as were used to crucify Our Lord!'

'Nay, Mam, not the same nails, but similar like.'

'And that made you decide? About being a blacksmith?' Jack asked, looking at Isaac, seeing him for the first time, not as a trouble-making small boy, but as a growing youth, with ideas and opinions of his own, and he nodded slowly as if in approval.

'Nay, not just that, Dad, but that were part of it. But you know, working with something that could last hundreds of years, well, it makes you think, don't it?' Isaac said, finding himself, for virtually the first time in his life, able to talk to his dad without the fear of a thrashing involved. 'You see, when you smelt iron ore with charcoal, with charcoal rather than with coke, it allows the iron to breathe.' His enthusiasm was taking flight. 'It's not softer, exactly, but more... It's got more life in it, it don't rust,' he finished lamely, knowing what he meant but unable to adequately express his feelings.

'Mmmmm, I see,' Jack murmured, as Isaac sat forward on the edge of his chair, almost wishing that he had said nothing at all. The disappointment of failure now would be crushing, and he cursed himself for allowing Molly Hindle to stoke up his dreams.

Jack puffed slowly on his pipe and even Mary grew apprehensive, her earlier certainty that Jack would agree evaporating with every puff of smoke, afraid that Jack was merely contemplating the easiest way to let the boy down.

Finally, Jack took his pipe out from his mouth and turned to Mary. 'What do you think, Mary?'

'The lad's dead set on it, Jack. Dead set. And I'd do anything to keep him from going underground, you know that. We can manage the money and whatever it takes, I'll go without, only please, Jack, please give him this one chance.'

'Thee goes without more than enough already, Mary, I'll not have no more on it,' he said, and her heart fell.

'Nay, Jack, there's always summat I can scrimp on.'

Jack scratched his chin as he thought for a short while. 'They have blacksmiths at the pit, thee knows, shoeing the galloways, the pit ponies, and making bits and pieces needed for the machinery. Have you thought of that? I could speak to Mr Baker, see if there's owt there?'

'It'd not be the same Dad, honest. Not the same as a proper apprenticeship with Mr Adlard. He makes all sorts down there, tools for farms, hinges for gates, fancy wrought-iron work, not just horse shoes and that. Working at t'pit... well, it would be just that, wouldn't it?'

'And he'd have to go underground, and you know how dead set against that I am, Jack. Not just for Isaac. For any of thee.'

'Well then, looks like I'd best be getting on down to see Henry Adlard... summat about an apprenticeship.'

'Ohhh, thanks, Dad. Thanks. Thanks! Don't know how else to say it, but thanks, Dad.'

'Aye, thank you, Jack, you don't know how much this means to me,' Mary said, feeling as though she could burst into song.

'Oh aye, but I do, Mary lass. I do.'

Isaac jumped up, his eyes shining with excitement, scarcely able to believe it had happened. He wanted to hug his mother and father out of sheer happiness, but did not know how to. 'I'll just be off for a minute, go and tell Molly, she'll be dead chuffed,' and he stopped in his tracks, his ears burning with embarrassment as he realised he had spoken of Molly.

'Molly?' his mother asked quizzically. 'Would that be Molly Hindle? Freda Hindle's lass?'

'Aye. That's her.'

'Courting are you then, lad?' Jack bellowed, with heavy humour.

'Nay Dad, nowt like that. She just helped me, that were all. She's interested like,' and Isaac fled before he could be interrogated further.

Mary crossed over to Jack's chair and put her hand on his shoulder. 'Thanks for that, Jack. You're a grand man and you've made our Isaac dead happy. He's a good lad and he'll make something out of himself now. Thanks to you.'

'I did it for thee, lass, as much as for the lad.'

'I know that Jack and I love thee for it.'

Jack tapped his pipe out again and leaned back in his chair, suddenly feeling very tired and sighed. 'Eh, I don't know, Mary, our Isaac seeing a lass. Where does the time go to, eh? Hardly seems like yesterday since him and Saul was born.'

'You know what this means, don't you, Jack? Isaac going to the forge? And seeing Molly Hindle? It means that he and Saul are starting to drift apart. They are not just "the twins" anymore; they're separate people now, in their own right.'

'Well, that's no bad thing. Isaac will do all the better for being out from under Saul's influence.'

Mary looked down at the *Daily Sketch* that Jack had laid aside after his dinner. Austria was mobilising against Serbia, Germany was sabre-rattling and the smell of war was heavy in the air, tangible and brooding, a thunderstorm waiting to break.

'I only hope all this talk of a war doesn't spoil things for him,' she said, 'change things too much.'

'Aye Mary, the world's going to change alright. There's no doubt about that, the world's changing. And I'm not so sure it's going to be a better place for it.'


*Isaac Garforth was duly apprenticed to Henry Adlard and started work on 26th June 1914.*

*On the 4th August, war between Great Britain and Germany broke out; the Great War, the war to end all wars, had begun. In early Octo-*

ber, Isaac's elder brother Edgar answered Kitchener's call to arms and volunteered.

Requisitioning officers from the Army scoured the country, buying and commandeering as many horses as they could (over 485,000 horses died on "active service" in France) and business at the forge quickly fell away. Without horses to shoe and with war austerity meaning that no fancy wrought-iron work was required, Henry Adlard could barely scratch a living. His assistant, Harry Spofforth, joined up and, in December 1914, so did he. The forge was closed up and Isaac Garforth's apprenticeship was terminated "for the duration".

Isaac joined his brother Saul, working down the mine.

In the summer of 1915, Edgar Garforth died on the beaches of Sulva Bay in Gallipoli and Isaac, now fifteen, tried to enlist. He was rejected, but tried again in December 1915 and then once more in June 1916. He had grown up and filled out, big for his age, and so a less than scrupulous recruiting Sergeant finally accepted him. After basic training, Isaac and several others were sent to the 14th Battalion of the Durham Light Infantry, as replacements for those lost on the Somme, particularly during the attack on Fricourt and at Bazentine Ridge.

Isaac saw action at Arras in early 1917 and then at the battle of Passchendaele in September 1917. During the attack on Polygon Wood, he was severely wounded, and his left arm had to be amputated. He was invalided out of the Army in February 1918.

With help from Molly, he did learn to write legibly with his right hand, but the dreams of the forge, the smells of the furnace and red-hot metal, the sweaty steam of horses waiting to be shod, the cascades of lucent tumbling sparks from the beaten iron, the crash of hammer on anvil and the fiery dragon's-breath of the furnace and bellows, they were gone forever, drowned in the mud of Passchendaele.


Only shadows of the dream remained.

# AS IT WAS, AS IT IS

Call me Bill. Just Bill. No other name necessary. Just Bill. That's how I've always been known.

My mother, however, insisted on calling me William, which I hated with a passion, so don't think that you can call me that – William.

Just Bill will do nicely – almost as one word – Justbill.

I think there was a character in a book I read once called Just Bill – but it wasn't me (wasn't one of the characters who confronts the murderous Pennywise the Clown in Stephen King's *IT* called Just Bill, or am I thinking of something else? – answers on a postcard please).

Anyway, I digress. So why are we here? I don't mean that in the metaphysical sense, as in why are have we been put on this planet and what is the greater cosmic picture and is there life after death and what is the meaning of life sort of way – I mean why are you and I sitting down having this little chat?

It's because of the reunion. I don't know whose stupid idea it was to hold the reunion, but the prospect of meeting up again – forty years later – with a bunch of people I didn't much like back then has to be one of the most insane suggestions since somebody suggested routing the *Titanic* through the middle of an icefield. Or suggesting that Donald Trump was a suitable candidate for the Presidency.

Let me explain. Forty long, glorious, fleet-footed years ago I was at University. Always enunciated with a capital U. University. Say it out loud with gravitas. *Univerrrrsity.*

Today, the kids call it Uni. but, in my time – to appropriate one of my mother's favourite expressions (as in 'in my time people had respect for their betters and in my time people knew their place and in my time respectable girls kept their knickers on and their knees closed) – in my time we called it, almost reverently, University. 'My William's going to University,' my mother would say proudly. Actually, she didn't say it with pride; being an inveterate snob for no good reason, she was mortally offended that I had not got into either Oxford or Cambridge, thus depriving her of the opportunity to boast to her church committee friends that 'My William's up at Oxford, you know, reading law.'

It would not have been so bad if I had chosen to study at one of the better non-Oxford or Cambridge Universities – Exeter or Durham, say – but instead I chose – *chose* – to go to the University of South Yorkshire, with its campus located in the not so charming mining and steel town of West Garside. Why it is called West Garside I have no idea. After all, there is no East, North or South Garside, so why West Garside? Don't bother sending your answers on a postcard for this one as I don't really want to know.

If you want to find the way to West Garside – not that I would recommend it –take the M1 from London and you will find West Garside to the north of Sheffield, to the south of Bradford and Leeds, to the east of Manchester and the west of Doncaster. Take all the worst elements of all those cities, lump them together – old heavy industries dead or dying, urban blight, sink housing estates, high unemployment, shuttered and graffiti-spattered shops, slums, pollution, crime and neglect – and there you have West Garside.

West Garside; my mother had never even heard of it and had to look it up in her RAC Road Atlas. (She chose membership of the RAC over the AA because it had Royal in its name – the Royal Automobile Club as opposed to the utterly plebeian Automobile Association.)

'Good heavens, William, do people, I mean *our* sort of people, actually live in places like that? In my time...'

Yes, Mother they do. Real people.

Anyway, I studied (probably too strong a word, "studied"; I occasionally attended lectures at USY. I was studying History and Geography and there are no prizes for guessing what I now do for a living with those highly vital qualifications – yes, I am a teacher) and, like every other normal student, spent the rest of my time getting drunk and trying to get laid – but I was infinitely more successful at the former than the latter.

For the first two terms of my fresher's year, I lived in the Arnold Durkin Hall of Residence. Arnold Durkin was a West Garside car trader who made a fortune importing Japanese cars when they were still absurdly cheap and held together with string and chewing gum and, having made his pile, decided to become a benefactor of his home-town University. Not that he actually lived in West Garside any more – no fool, he. As soon as he had made his money, he buggered off to the Bahamas and has not set foot in the place since except to officially open the Residence in a joint ribbon-cutting ceremony with the Lady Mayoress of West Garside, the redoubtable Mrs Margaret Boothroyd who, legend has it, once worked as Arnold's secretary and turned down an offer of marriage from Arnold to marry Gerald Boothroyd JP, one of West Garside's wealthiest businessman, instead.

Arnold was at that time a small garage owner with grease under his fingernails and bad breath. Gerald Boothroyd lost most of his money a few years later whilst Arnold Durkin went on to make a pile. But he still had bad breath. Whether Mrs Boothroyd ever regretted her decision not to marry the soon-to-be-fabulously-wealthy Arnold Durkin is not recorded. But since Arnold subsequently married Margaret's best friend Freda and Margaret divorced Gerald shortly after his fall from fortune, we may draw our own conclusions.

The Arnold Durkin Hall of Residence sticks out from the hilly slopes of Burnside Road, on the south side of West Garside, like an inflated wart on the end of a bulbous nose. If there was a prize for the ugliest architecture ever built – not just in West Garside, not just in South Yorkshire, not just in England, Great Britain, Europe or wherever – the worldwide Nobel Prize for Bad Architecture, the Arnold Durkin Hall of Residence for the University of South Yorkshire would win without the need for a recount. It is UGLY. And in a town as ugly as West Garside, believe you me, that takes some doing. That takes genius.

The walls are built from the vilest shiny yellow bricks you ever saw, with spandrel panels below the slit-eyed windows of such a vile shade of fluorescent green you need sunglasses, a sort of dayglow-diarrhoea colour. The windows are out of proportion to the scale of the elevations, little more than strips of glass, as if the brickie had decided to miss out a few bricks at the end of his shift.

The entire building sits like a squat, bad-tempered toad in a sea of dirty asphalt, its cantilevered arse-end (the toilet and shower block) hanging over the car park like an avalanche waiting to happen. The accommodation cells – one hesitates to use the word rooms – are so small and oddly proportioned, long and narrow, with slit windows, that it was like living in the middle of a railway tunnel with that faint glimmer of light in the distance which indicates the tunnel's end.

Freezing cold in winter, baking hot in summer, the Arnold Durkin Halls of Residence were not a pleasant place to live. By the way, Jim Potson, the architect who also designed most of the other new campus buildings, was later jailed for massive corruption, offering bribes to council officials all over the north of England to put commissions his way. He should have been incarcerated in his own creation – now, that would have been poetic justice!

Which is why, for the third term of my first year, I moved out of Durkin Hall and took digs with Mrs Greenbaum in Black-shank Avenue, down and around the corner from Burnside Road. Although I stayed at Mrs Greenbaum's for almost twelve weeks, I never did get to count exactly how many cats there were. They were everywhere. Now don't get me wrong, I like cats (the Ming Dynasty Chinese takeaway in Clanmore Road does a very nice sweet and sour – its motto, *So many cats – So many recipes*), but not absolutely everywhere. And especially not crawling all over my living quarters shedding hairballs and cat-turds all over the place.

I got up of a morning, usually thick-headed from the previous night's drinking and had to run a gauntlet of mewling moggies as I headed for the bathroom on the first floor landing, stepping delicately through a minefield of rank cat litter trays and those extra little sticky, squidgy brown parcels where the cat had not quite made it to the litter tray in time. Sometimes I made it to the bathroom with my feet unsullied, other times not.

God, the place stank like a zoo on a hot summer's day. What am I talking about? The place *was* a zoo!

As I say, I never did get to count them all, but I did get to recognise some of the more regular ones. One of them was a great, shabby, tabby tom, as big as a small dog, called Budge. He was called Budge because wherever you wanted to sit down, Budge was there, wherever you walked on the stairs Budge was there, wherever you went, Budge was there, in your way. He got told to budge off out of it so often, he came to think that Budge was his name.

Budge had one ear badly chewed away from his numerous catfights inside and outside the menagerie and was so mean and ugly-looking, you were bound to think he must be top-cat at Mrs Greenbaum's. Don't you believe it. That honour went to a pretty little white female called Lucy, so delicate and fragile you would think she would fall apart in your hands if you tried to pick her up – not that she would ever let you, she would claw your eyes out in a flash if you tried.

Lucy (probably short for Lucyfur?) ruled the roost and no mistake. Whilst she held court on the stairs, no other cat dared to come near her, not even Budge, who slunk away from her with his tail curled beneath his hind legs in submission. Her eyes, a soft liquid violet in colour, held so much malevolence you would swear she was a devil-cat. Her hate-filled, unblinking gaze followed you around, evil oozing from her like a thick green miasma.

It was early one evening, only a couple of weeks after I moved in, that I first crossed Lucy. Coming down from the bathroom in my dressing gown and slippers, towel over my arm and washbag in hand, Lucy was on the stairs beneath me, back towards me, surveying her kingdom. Her tail twitched softly from side to side. Lucy knew I was behind her, but I was so far beneath her contempt that she did not even bother to look towards me as I put my foot down onto the step beside her. Her tail flicked against my bare foot and, quick as a flash, she spat, hissed, clawed me down my Achilles Heel and sank her needle-sharp teeth into my calf, all in a fluid motion which would have been admirable to watch if it had not been so bloody painful.

'Vot you do?' Mrs. Greenbaum screeched at me from the bottom of the stairs. 'You kick my Lucy.'

'No, honestly, I didn't touch her, her tail just flicked, and she bit me. Look she's brought blood.'

'You muz be torment her,' she continued, wagging a scrawny finger me. 'Von more such zing you hurt my darlinks and out you goes. And no refund on monies paid. You just vatch me. I zink you goot boy, now I knows you pussy-killer. I call ze police and RSPCA.'

'And I'll call the Health Inspector,' I answered back in a flash. But only under my breath as, vile as it was at Mrs Greenbuam's, I had nowhere else to go. I would sleep on the benches in Blonk

Street Bus Station before going back to Durkin Hall, so I held my tongue whilst Lucy simpered at Mrs Greenbaum and then glanced back to glare at me with raw hatred.

After that, Lucy mounted a concerted campaign against me – I swear this is so.

Even though I would religiously lock my door before going out, the cats still got into my room. How, I don't know. They left dead mice on my pillow or clean clothes, thoughtfully chewed into intestinally-spilling little parcels.

Other times, they peed in the corner, they walked across my table and crumpled up my course work papers. Sometimes, if they were feeling particularly malevolent towards me, they would shit on my work; constructive literary criticism I can take, but I didn't need some scuzzy furball to tell me quite so graphically that my paper on the effects of the Industrial Revolution on Rural Habitats was crap. And I would swear that Lucy knew, just knew, when the paper had to be submitted and would wait until the last possible moment before befouling it, so that there was no time to rewrite. She would sit on the stairs with that knowing smug smile on her face, tail twitching from side to side, watching me as I discovered her little present, still hot and steaming, carefully deposited on my work.

Complaints to Mrs Greenbaum were a waste of breath. 'No, no Mr Justbill, not my little darlinks, you muz' be z'aggerating, or maybe you bring in dog muck on your shoes, you muz' alvays vipe your shooss on ze mat. Not y'genic to bring ze dog muck inside, my little darlinks are so delicate, not good for ze y'gene.'

Then she would launch into a long, rambling diatribe about how she and her husband Franz (long since dead, probably from some-feline borne disease) had barely escaped from Nazi Germany, how all her relatives and Franz's relatives had died in the concentration camps and how lucky I was to live in a free country and how I must not abuse that freedom by accusing her 'poor innocent leetle darlinks of such dirty zings'.

How I wished I could escape, but I had paid my term's rent in advance and could not afford to move anywhere else.

And as if the cat-harassment-campaign was not enough, there was the question of the food. My rent was supposed to cover for two meals a day, breakfast and evening dinner. Lunch, I would take in the college canteen, or at Kostis's Kostless Greek Restaurant across the road.

The food served up by Mrs Greenbaum I cannot describe, but suffice it to say that the stuff that came out of tins and was dollopped onto the numerous unwashed cat feeding bowls that were scattered around, looked considerably more appetising than that which was put before me and the two other unfortunate tenants who had unwittingly stepped into this feline-spattered nightmare, one of whom you shall meet later. And if, for some unknown reason, you were unable to eat all of this delightful repast, not to worry, you would get it served up again the next night. And the night after that. Only when the mould on the food became indistinguishable from the cat hairs would it be thrown away.

So, for my sophomore and final years I decided to look for rooms in a shared student house. As soon as I got back to West Garside for the autumn term, I took a temporary room in the YMCA hostel on Greystones Avenue whilst waiting for my friend, Peter Coulbourne, to turn up and then find somewhere to live.

Peter and I were taking the same courses and, as he had had a similar digs horror story, we decided next term to share student accommodation somewhere (but separate rooms, you understand, Peter was not that kind of friend). In his case, the landlord from hell, Mr Caunt, used to patrol the corridors at night to ensure that none of his guests somehow lost their sense of direction and accidentally found themselves in another student's room. All lights had to be out by 10 o'clock and after 10.30, the front door was locked and bolted, not to be opened again under any circumstances until 7.30 the following morning.

Hot water was rationed to an hour in the morning and an hour in the evening. Food there was at least edible, but of such minute quantities that Peter was always hungry. Even an extra slice of toast had to be paid for and as for second helpings, forget it; there was barely a first helping.

I had expected Peter to be back at West Garside at the beginning of term time, but when he did not turn up, I thought he had been temporarily delayed, possibly had the 'flu or something. Which is why I did not start looking for somewhere for a week or more – though, by the Wednesday of the second week, I was getting a bit concerned. I had lost his phone number and could only remember that he lived somewhere in Essex – Colchester? Chelmsford? I tried directory enquiries and, after a few false starts and lots of coins fed in the voraciously greedy pay phone, finally tracked him down.

'Hello, er, sorry to bother you but is that Mrs Coulborne, the mother of Peter, Peter Coulbourne, who's a student at USY, West Garside?'

'Yes?' A very wary and cautious reply.

'Ah, well, the thing is, this is his friend Bill, Just Bill, at USY too… and I … er… Peter and me, we were going to room together but… er… he doesn't seem to have come back this term. Is Peter there at all?'

'Yes, er… Bill. Peter did mention you, although his father and I didn't know he intended to room with you, Bill. Peter made no mention of that at all.'

'Is Peter coming back to West Garside, Mrs Coulbourne? Is he there, can I talk to him?'

'I'm afraid not, Bill.'

'When will he be back? I really do need to talk to him to make arrangements and that?'

'Oh dear, this is so terribly hard. You see, Bill, our daughter Jennifer, she was killed a car crash, soon after the summer break started. Peter and Jennifer were so very close…' I could hear her voice breaking up, the pain of her grief beginning to overwhelm her.

'Oh... I am so... so sorry.' What can you say? Anything, everything, sounds so trite and meaningless.

'Peter... Peter could not face going back to... to...'

'I understand, Mrs Coulborne, I really am very sorry. And please pass on my condolences to Peter.'

'Peter's gone, Bill. He packed a bag and left, he called us from Dover. He... he is going to go to India... To find some peace, he said. With some guloo or whatever you call them.'

'Guru.'

'Yes, guloo. So, we've lost them, you see. Jennifer and Peter both.'

'I am sorry to have disturbed you. Thank you for telling me, Mrs Coulbourne, I won't take up any more of your time.'

The poor, distraught woman put the phone down without responding, and who can blame her.

So, two weeks into term I had to find somewhere to live, acutely conscious that all the best accommodation would already have been taken

However, the University lodgings officer seemed a likely place to start.

Mr Bream, the lodgings officer, occupied a small, cluttered office in the further reaches of the admin block in the main college building (also designed by the jailed Jim Potson in a style best described as post-modern brutalist monumentalism... in other words, nobody gave a stuff how the building worked inside as long as it looked impressive from the outside – which it didn't).

Past the main reception desk, along a dark corridor (without doors or windows), up a half flight of stairs that led nowhere, down a half flight of stairs that led nowhere, round two corners, one going left, followed by one going right. Pant your way up another flight of stairs, along a landing, past locked doors that apparently had no handles and through the door at the end of the passage. Then down another long corridor – past one or two skeletons of former students who had got lost and perished as they wandered up and down the endless passages – before finally debouching at the bottom of yet another long flights of steps and, not more than two corners further on, to arrive at the offices of the said Mr Bream.

Mr Bream was a short, crumpled man, long since gone to lard, who evidently decided that the Bobby Charlton comb-over look – seven or eight strands of mousy hair carefully glued down across a liver-spotted pate – combined with a polyester suit in shiny royal blue, a crumpled check shirt and egg-stained tie, was going to have dozens of nubile female students desperate for lodgings drooling all over him. Plain Fay, who also found her lodgings through Bream, said he made her flesh creep as he leered and slurped a greasy white tongue over his lips and said, 'Lots of student parties and orgies, eh, Fay? You'll invite me, won't you, eh lass? 'Specially as I've tekken such good care to find you summat suitable,' while leaning over his desk to try and see her legs.

Shit, he made my flesh creep, yet alone Plain Fay's.

Bream's rat-hole of an office reeked of stale sweat and tobacco and I was beginning to wish I'd tried to find somewhere from the small ads in the *West Garside Chronicle* as Bream made a great show of getting up from his desk, crossing over to the battered filing cabinet and flipping through files; even from across the desk I could see the drawer only held about a dozen files which he flicked through one after another and then back to the first one again, as if searching for that one special property ideally suited for only me.

Back to his desk – shuffle through some papers – back to his filing cabinet, slurping on his yellow teeth as he flipped through the same files for the fifth time. This time, he did pull out a file, laid it down on his desk and sat himself back into his chair with a solid, meaty thump. The poor chair creaked with righteous indignation. Bream, I noticed, had an inch-long, thick, silver hair growing out from the bottom of his right ear lobe, as if he were wearing an earring made from polished silver wire. I could barely resist the temptation to reach across and pluck it out, just to see him wince.

As if about to take the reading from the Bible at Sunday morning service, Bream reverently opened his blue cardboard file and scanned over the single sheet of paper which was all that the folder contained.

'Aye, there we has it, sonny, the very beast. No 66 Vernon Road, very nice accommodation, even if I says so myself. I've seen dozens an' dozens of student places in me time, lad, I can tell thee, but this is one of the best. If not *the* best. Been savin' this'un for somebody as'll appreciate it, like. Mr Clears, the land-lord, e's been on us books for yonks. 'E only lives next door, no 68, any complaints, problems, owt, he'll fix it in a twinkling of an eyebrow.

'Right reasonable rates an' all, lad, I'll give him a bell right now and tell him you're on t'way to look it out. E'll want 'is term's rent in advance, of course. Soon as your grant cheque's cleared, sonny, you can pay him right off and move in. Very discreet, too, is Mr Clears...' Bream leered, tapping the side of his nose with a nicotine-stained finger, 'if tha' knows what I means. Parties, girls, tha' knows? Turn a blind eye, 'e will, but you just tip me the wink, sonny and I'll come and join thee. I'll show these college lasses a thing or two, I can tell thee. Still life in the old dog yet, you know, sonny.'

'Call me "sonny" once more and the question of whether there's any life left in you might be open to debate.'

'All reet, all reet, there's no need to get shirty, I'm only doing me chuffing best to get you fixed up, no need for all that aggression.'

I took down the details. The rent seemed reasonable, and even though I would have to provide all my food, I still reck-oned I could just about get by provided I ate no more than once a fortnight. Besides, I was running out of options.

On the way back from the lodging office, I came across Stanley Bernstein.

Which was how I came to be sharing No 66 Vernon Road, commonly known as Vermin House, with five other escapees from either the Arnold Durkin Hall of Detention, or other bed-sit horrors, such as Mrs Greenbaum's.

Vernon Road was a short bus ride up from the University, appropriately the No. 66 bus. The Nettles, the pub on the corner of Vernon Road and Sideways Down (I kid you not) is your land-mark; the bus stop is fifty yards or so past. Why the pub is called The Nettles nobody knows, but I did hear it suggested that it was because the best bitter tasted as though it had been brewed from them.

Jump off the bus, turn back towards the Nettles and just before you reach Sideways Down, number 66 is on your left hand side, the second from the end before you reach Sideways Down. No 68, the home of Mr Clears, the landlord, is on the corner.

One of a long row of terrace houses, built from bricks that might once have been red but were now so coated with grime from the constant traffic, pollution, one hundred and fifty years'-worth of congealed coal-smoke soot from before the Clean Air Act (clean air in West Garside?) and general neglect and non-maintenance, any semblance of the original colour is probably illusory.

The ground floor front room has a bow window looking out onto a six foot by ten foot patch of compacted weeds surrounded by a low stone wall, topped with a row of short, spiked wrought iron railings.

The front door is to the left of the window. Two painted metal numbers are screwed to the green-painted woodwork of the door. However, one of the screws to the right hand sign – the six of 66 – has fallen out, so that the 6 has revolved through 90 degrees and looks like a 9. Number 69. The regular postman knew the correct number, of course, as did the paper boy who delivered Beerstain's *Times* and Gobbo's *Daily Worker*. But occasionally a relief postman got confused, which is how we came to know that Mr J. Ripper at No 69 was into mail-order gay porn.

It was Gobbo who opened the packet – by accident, he said, but nobody believed him. He probably thought of it as an act of anarchy; very big on anarchy and the class war, was Gobbo.

'Eh, luke at this, the dirty booger, 'im at no 69, orderin' this stuff thru' post!' Gobbo said at dinner, flashing around a wallet of photos showing naked men engaged in various homosexual acts. 'Ow'd you fancy this one eh, Slaney, big chopper like that?' pushing a photo into her face of a muscular body builder about to penetrate a youth who was bent over before him.

Slaney, forkful of stew almost into her mouth, dropped her fork onto her plate and glared at Gobbo. 'Jesus, Gobbo, that is so disgusting. And so are you, and anyway, what're you doing opening other folk's mail?'

'It's only pervy stuff, Slaney. Shouldn't be allowed.'

Disgusted, both with the unknown Mr J Ripper and with Gobbo, she snatched the photos from him as little flares of indignant colour crept across the back of her neck. 'Eh, give them back', he protested, 'I can sell them buggers down the Hussars.' (West Garside's gay pub, situated on the corner of Mulberry Street, was, appropriately enough, called the Gay Hussars.)

'You'll do no such thing, Gobbo. You can't just go round opening other folk's mail, you'll go to jail, so you will. That's the Royal Mail, it's sort of like treason to tamper with other people's letters, even if it is vile filth like this. I'll burn the lot and put something decent in and push it through the letterbox and nobody will be any the wiser. He'll think he's been conned or cheated and won't dare complain.'

Not even deigning to look at the photos, holding them face down, Slaney set a match to them over the almost empty saucepan of stew we had been eating, the acrid smoke of burning photographic paper catching at our throats.

'Hold on,' protested Gobbo, determined to salvage some lost ground, 'there's still some stew left. I wanted that.'

'Tough,' she said, continuing to burn the photos, only dropping them into the pan after they were completely incinerated, burning the tips of her fingers as she did so.

Gobbo, feigning anger, stomped up from the table and marched out. No doubt he had a protest rally somewhere to go to; very big on protest rallies, was Gobbo.

Slaney repacked the envelope with some religious tracts that had also been pushed through the door and added some photos of cows and sheep that Plain Fay had cut from a magazine as part of a collage she was making for an art project and then delivered it herself to No 69. Who knows, maybe Mr J Ripper got turned on by the photos of sheep instead?

All of which is yet another sidetrack.

We had got as far as the front door when we were momentarily diverted by the revelations of Mr Ripper's sexual predilections. You also briefly met up with Gobbo and Slaney, but I'll make a proper introduction shortly. For now, let us enter the house.

The front door squeals a bit as you pushed it open; Mr Clears never quite got round to oiling the hinges, no matter how many times he promised he would. The hallway is long and dingy; even in daylight, it looks dark and doomy, never enough light. (Mr Clears only ever used a single 40 watt bulb in the ceiling fitting and none of us were ever going to put our hands in our pockets to buy brighter light bulbs from our grants.)

The stairs are ahead of you, but we are not going upstairs just yet. There is a spindly-legged console table, the legs always loose and wobbly, the table always on the edge of collapse. Whoever is up first in the morning, or whoever is first back in the arvo if we have all gone to college before the post arrives, picks up our mail and puts it on the table and sometimes post that isn't even ours finds its way there as well.

The wallpaper along the hall, from the skirting to the dado

rail, is a heavy, textured paper, embossed with fleur de lys, that has been painted over in dark chocolate brown gloss paint. Above the dado there was, and probably still is, a cream paper long since turned brown from tobacco smoke, grease, hand-marks and general neglect.

The room to your right, the bow-fronted front room, was our sitting room, usually in a state of total disarray. One of the girls, usually Slaney, would try and keep it tidy, but her efforts usually only lasted about ten minutes – although having said that, Beer-stain was clean and tidy, and he did remonstrate with us to try and keep it less like a herd of stampeding water buffalo had just passed through. Gobbo would usually tell him to fuck off and then toss an empty beer can into the corner just to make his point.

A rented TV stood on a low table in the corner, an indoor aerial perched precariously on top like an alien spider waiting to pounce. Beerstain liked to watch obscure French and Italian movies on BBC 2, but the rest of us, excluding the girls, only ever wanted to watch sport. The girls liked quiz shows and costume dramas, the upshot being that none of us could ever agree what channel to put on and so, often as not, we would listen to music instead. (For the younger ones of you, and you will find this hard to believe, in those days there were only three TV channels, BBC1 and 2 and ITV, and they were in black and white, colour not having been invented yet.)

A battered three-seater sofa stood against the far wall, springs and stuffing long since given up the ghost so that all occupants invariably slid towards the centre. Another two-seat settee was placed across the bow window, whilst a battered brown leather armchair occupied the other corner. Provided we were all cosy with each other, the six of us could just about sit in there. But Gobbo's personal hygiene being what it was, nobody actually wanted to get cosy with him and so he usually sat in the armchair.

One day, Slaney went down to the second-hand furniture

mart on Lamb-bone Lane, behind the canal, and bought two large beanbags and carried them home on the bus, one tucked under each arm like bright blue pigs. Max Beerstain usually sat in one and Slaney on the other. At which Gobbo appropriated the three-seater settee, stretching himself out like the long streak of uselessness that he was, leaving Faye and Jane to the other settee and me to the armchair. Not that there were many occasions when we were all in Vermin House at the same time.

An old, battered, very heavy mahogany sideboard with lions-claw feet completed the furniture ensemble. A cheaply framed print of Van Gogh's Sunflowers had once hung over the sideboard, but we soon took that down and hung some of Faye's paintings instead. Bloody good there were, too; quite put Van Gogh to shame.

An archway to the left leads into the kitchen dining room and believe me, you really don't want to go in there, but if you insist....

Have a look at the cranking old refrigerator. Stuck to the door are Sellotaped lists and rosters, all prepared by Slaney.

*Monday – Shopping Max and Faye. Cleaning Jane and Gobbo. Cooking Bill and Slaney. Washing up Max and Jane.*

*Tuesday – Shopping Jane and Gobbo, Cleaning Bill and Slaney. Cooking Max and Faye. Washing up – Jane and Gobbo.*

And so on through the week. Nobody took the slightest bit of notice. Gobbo was always noticeably missing whenever it was his turn to shop. Or clean. Or cook. And especially washing up. Not that he minded eating if anyone else cooked. Otherwise, he would just take himself down to the chippie and not bother to bring any back for anyone else. On the rare occasions when he was actually forced to cook, he invariably produced chip butties, much to the disgust of Slaney, who was trying to lose weight. In case you are interested, my speciality was *boeuf bourguinon avec champignons* – beef and mushroom stew to you and me.

So, we'll give the kitchen no more than a cursory glance, note the pile of dirty dishes in the sink and move on. A back door leads out into a communal yard shared by eight of the houses, entered by a passage between No. 64 and No. 62.

Back into the house again, past the kitchen into the hallway once more and on to the staircase. Be careful on the stairs, the stair carpet is old and worn, especially on the sixth tread down from the half landing. Here, the nap is worn through to the jute backing and it is easy to catch your heel in the enlarging hole. (Complaints to Mr Clear, the landlord, were always to no avail. 'Good as new', he'd say. 'Only bin laid a year or two, plenty of good wear and tear in it yet, nay bother.')

At the half landing you will find the bathroom – the door half glazed with frosted glass (and on more than one occasion the girls have caught Gobbo trying to peer through when one of them is taking a bath – or perhaps he was simply trying to observe how a bath is actually used, as his acquaintance with bathing seems limited).

The bathroom is actually not too shabby, being a recent addition as Vermin House did not originally boast such an amenity. There is a claw-footed enamel bath which is fairly regularly cleaned by Faye and Slaney, a standard issue washbasin and a toilet – a bit stained, and very smelly after Gobbo has been in, but not too bad. A Jubilee Day bunting of washing is permanently draped across the retractable washing line over the bath – bras panties, pants, socks, T-shirts (but vary rarely anything of Gobbo's, whose philosophy on washing clothes, especially socks, is 'why bother, they're only goin' to get fuckin' dirty again.').

Continuing round from the bathroom, we come to the first floor landing. There are three bedrooms at this level. Vermin House is actually much larger and roomier inside than it would appear to be from the exterior. The two bedrooms at the rear are occupied by Max Beerstain and me, the shit-hole at the front is Gobbo's. If you must go into Gobbo's room, make sure to shut the door behind you else his socks try to escape again. Gobbo's room is the biggest and best in the house – the master bedroom – but as he was here first, I supposed he was entitled to his pick.

Carry on up the stairs to the second level and you'll find Slaney's room at the front, i.e. directly over Gobbo, whilst Plain Faye and Jane have the back two rooms – not that Jane is ever there much. These rooms are up in the roof space; they have less headroom and partly pitched ceilings and the windows are gabled, but the girls do make them cosy.

So, there you have it, the guided tour – cream tea and scones are now available in the drawing room and don't forget to exit via the gift shop for that extra special souvenir – one of Gobbo's socks perhaps?

Maybe I'll tell you happened next.

But most probably not.

# AN ACT OF SUBVERSION

'You there! Get in here, sit there and don't speak.'

'But I don't understand, why, why have I been brought here?'

'I said, sit there and don't speak.'

'But what...why? Why?'

'Are you hard of hearing or just stupid? Sit down and do not say a word until spoken to.'

'But...?'

'I said sit; even the stupidest dog understands that. Sit down.'

'OK, I'll sit but please tell me who you are and why I'm in here?'

'I am OT Sergeant Painstaking of the State Bureau of Investigative Criminal Procedures and I am to investigate your crimes, of course, that's why.'

'The SBICP, the secret police?'

'The State Bureau is not secret, we have no secrets, it is the secret subversive behaviour of others that concern us. '

'I'm sorry, Sergeant Painstaking, but I don't know what your title, OT, stands for. Something important, I am sure.'

'OT? I am an Official Torturer, of course,

'Official torturer? Oh, my God! Torture? No!'

'Yes, it is a necessary procedure in the investigation of crime.

Don't worry, the marks and scars are rarely permanent, but torture is essential for the proper scrutiny into crimes. Crimes such as yours.'

'Crimes? What crimes?'

'That is what we are here to investigate, isn't it? Crimes such as subversion.'

'What subversion? I've never been subversive. Ever.'

'Maligning the State is a serious crime, very serious.'

'But I haven't. I... I don't... don't malign the State, ever.'

'So you say.'

'I do, most certainly.'

'We shall see. Now! Your name! Tell me your name!'

'If you are supposedly investigating me, you already know my name, don't you?'

'Refusing to give your name to an officer of the State is a serious crime. Another serious crime!'

'I'm not refusing, just I... Alright, my name is Alice Munro.'

'You lie! You are lying!'

'What do you mean, I'm lying? Of course Alice Munro *is my* name.'

'No, your name is Susannah Alice Patricks. Not Alice Munro. Giving a false name is an offence.'

'I was born Susannah Alice Patricks, certainly, but I never liked the name Susannah and, from being a child, I asked everyone to call me Alice. And Patricks is my maiden name, it changed to Munro when I married Peter, Peter Munro, my husband.'

'Yes, Peter Munro, he is also under investigation.'

'Peter! For what?'

'He is ideologically unsound.'

'Ideologically unsound? What on earth does that means when it's at home?'

'He does not fully endorse the ideology of the State. That is subversion.'

'Subversion?'

'Absolutely. Subversion.'

'How can Peter be subversive? He works for the State.'

'Subversion exists everywhere, in all the unlikeliest places.'

'He's an English teacher. How can that be subversive, for God's sake?'

'By teaching seditious and subversive texts.'

'That's silly. The only texts he is allowed to teach are those of the approved curriculum: *The Exalted Life of the Glorious Leader, Great Thoughts of the Glorious Leader, More Great Thoughts of the Glorious Leader, Wonderful Life-Affirming Thoughts of the Glorious Leader, The Glorious Leader Dictionary, The Glorious Leader's Easy Quilting and Embroidery* and *The Glorious Leader's Five-Year Plan to achieve World Domination*. Wonderful and uplifting works such as those.'

'However, it is how he teaches such great works; he can teach them in a sarcastic, subversive, negative manner.'

'No, not by Peter. Definitely not. He is a dedicated teacher and fully subscribes to the thoughts of the Glorious Leader. One of his favourites is *'Teaching peasants to read is like teaching fish to climb mountains'*, a pointless exercise and therefore forbidden. He really does believe in that.'

'But he grows his hair long, doesn't he? He is just the type, rebellious, sloppy and disrespectful.'

'No, no, he has his hair cut exactly in the same manner as the Glorious Leader; it is so flattering and makes him look so handsome. Just like the Glorious Leader. And you, of course.'

'Commendable loyalty, such a shame that you are not so loyal to the State. The Glorious Leader also said, *'a moth seeks light, not enlightenment, I am the only path to enlightenment.'* I also seek enlightenment. You have yet to enlighten me that you are absolutely devoted to the State.'

'I am, I am. Really I am.'

'You do not convince. Why did you invoke the name of God, who is of course non-existent? Why did you not instead invoke the name of the Glorious Leader? Not to do so is disrespectful and denying his magnificence is a crime.'

'I'm sorry, it was a thoughtless slip of the tongue, I meant no disrespect to our Glorious Leader, long may he shine his glorious light upon us all.'

'There is a lack of conviction in your protestations.'

'I'm just nervous, that's all.'

'Nervous? Why are you nervous? An innocent person would not be nervous. Only the guilty have reasons to be nervous.'

'Confused then, not nervous.'

'Confused? Confusion denotes uncertainty, uncertainty as to the righteousness of the State and rejection of the ideology.'

'No, no, the State is always right in everything.'

'That is true; the State is absolute, as is the Glorious Leader.'

'Those are my sentiment exactly, Sergeant Painstaking.'

'You are how old? What's your date of birth?

'23 Somenda in the 54th Year of our Glorious Leader's rule. I'm thirty-seven years old.'

'How many children?'

'We have no children… despite…'

'Why not? Why do you have no children? It is mandatory for all parents to have a minimum of two children. Why have you disobeyed this imperative State regulation?'

'We have tried – oh, how we have tried! We have had every possible treatment going, been poked and prodded, blood tests by the score… believe me, there is nothing we would have liked more than to have had children'

'That will be checked out. Address! Give me your address.'

'What?'

'Your address. And no more lies.'

'74, North I Street, in the 7th Glorious Leader District.'

'Why?'

'Why… what?'

'Why 74 North Street?'

'Because… because it's a nice house, a nice house at a price we could afford.'

'No! It's because it is close to a military establishment, isn't it?'

'What military establishment? There is no military establishment anywhere near.'

'How do you know there is no military establishment unless you have looked for one? You looked for a military establishment nearby to spy on it, didn't you? Spying is a capital offence.'

'No, no, nothing like that. Why would you say that?'

'If you did not go looking for military secrets, how did you know there aren't any, eh? Answer me that.'

'I can't. I mean, it's so bizarre. How can you prove a negative? A double negative. It's such twisted logic. Whatever answer I give is going to be wrong, isn't it?'

'So you are deliberately lying, giving me wrong answers.'

'No, no, it's not that, but I can't prove to you that I did not look for a house close to a military establishment. Maybe we chose the house precisely because it was *not* close to such a place, so as to avoid the possibility of accusations of spying.'

'Now you are playing semantics. Answer the question and stop prevaricating. Prevaricating to a State official is an offence. Answer the question.'

'What question? You haven't asked a question. Just made some vague accusations. '

'The State does not make accusations without justification.'

'I… I realise that, that the State is inevitably infallible, but… I don't know how to answer you.'

'Give me the names of your associates. Who are they? Names.'

'Associates? Associates at work? I'm a part-time junior accountant. I add up columns of figures, give them to a more senior accountant who adds up and checks the same list and *he* then gives the list to the next person up the ladder for checking again. Hardly any world-shattering secrets there, are there?'

'You are being facetious. I will not tolerate facetiousness.'

'Yes... I mean no, I'm sorry. Please, what was your question again?'

'I want the names of your associates in subversion.'

'Subversion? I don't have any associates in subversion, truthfully, Sergeant Painstaking.'

'So! You operate on your own, spreading subversion and sedition. If you have no associates, you must operate alone, is that not so?'

'Oh, this is so bizarre; it's like something from Kafka. Kafkaesque.'

'Kafka? Kafka? Who is this Kafka, your partner in subversion?'

'No, no, he's an author.'

'A writer! All writing is forbidden, all reading is forbidden apart from the works of the Glorious Leader, you know that. Associating with a writer is sedition.'

'Kafka is dead, how can I associate with him?'

'You killed him to avoid discovery, to conceal your subversive activities with him, isn't that it?'

'No, Franz Kafka has been dead for... I don't know – sixty, seventy, maybe a hundred years.'

'But you must have read his forbidden books to be able to say that this legally constituted interrogation is like Kafka.'

'I... I read his works many years before the Great Banning. Before the Great Burning of Books.'

'But what do you mean when you say "like Kafka. Kafkaesque"?'

'Kafka wrote a story about a nameless man who is arrested and tried by a remote authority and is never told what his supposed crime is, and the reader is never told, either. He also wrote a weird story about a man who turns himself into a cockroach or some other such hideous creature.'

'And how is that relevant, Kafkaesque?'

'Well, I have been summoned here, held here and I don't

what I am supposed to have done. What my alleged offences are.'

'I told you. Subversive, sedition and maligning the State. Serious, serious crimes.'

'But that's so general, generic, it's like a doctor telling a patient he is ill without specifying the illness.'

'It's not for you to know, only to admit your guilt.'

'What guilt? This has to be sort of mistake, a very serious mistake.'

'The State is absolute; you have admitted as such. The State does not make mistakes. To accuse the State, and by implication the Glorious Leader, of a mistake is a serious and criminal offence. An act of subversion. Susannah Alice Munro, you are under arrest.'

# AN ONLY SON

And she a widow.
(St Luke)

'Ehh, you must be right proud of your Dennis,' Emma Arkwright said, weighing out the onions. 'I mean, going up to London like that to become a doctor an' all. It were what you always wanted for t'lad, weren't it?'

'It was his own decision,' Susan Broadbent answered, rather more defensively than she had intended.

'Oh aye, I'm sure, no doubt, but ever since he were a little sprout you was on at him, always telling him. "Dennis," you'd say, "when you grow up, you're going to be a doctor!" And now he is and so I say, you must be right proud of him.'

'He's only just started first year medical studies.'

'Aye, so he'll be away for years yet, then?'

He was an only son,

Susan Broadbent wished that Emma Arkwright would shut up and mind her own business. As well as selling groceries and newspapers, Arkwright's shop was also the village gossip exchange, with every item of local gossip or scandal polished and garnished with Emma Arkwright's especial malignant spite. 'I always remember that time at the Church Fete,' Emma continued. 'You remember, when Bishop Waring come to give out the prizes? When were that?'

'I really can't recall.'

'Course you do! Anyhow, as I were saying, that time when Bishop Waring come to give out the prizes, although how he come t'give the prize to that slut Mildred Holden for that embroidery sampler, I shall never know. Anyhow, he were walking around, saying 'owdo and that and 'e stops to chat to you and Dennis – Helen Cantley were dead jealous, I remember that – and t'Bishop, 'e says to Dennis, "And what are you going to be when you grow up, young man?" Nobbut but five nor six 'e' was, and before he can open his little mouth, you say, "'E's going to be a doctor, aren't you, Dennis?" You must remember, surely?'

'No, really, I can't say that I do, Mrs Arkwright.'

'Course you do. Which is why I say you must be dead proud of him. Doing exactly what you want. I mean, I wish my Brian were like that. I wanted him to come and work for me in the shop, give me a hand, like, but no, off he went and got that job in Manchester. Still, when a lad's got a bit of a spark, you can't expect him to do everything his mam wants, can you?' She smiled benignly, as if unaware of the bitchiness of her remark.

Much against her will, Susan held her tongue.

'But did he have to go to London?' Emma carried on. 'I mean, you'd 'ave thought he'd 'ave gone somewhere local, wouldn't you, what with you being a widow an' all? You'd have thought he'd want to come home at weekends, give you a hand, like, on the farm?'

*Like your Brian does?* Susan thought, but kept it to herself. 'He went to London because that's the best there is. He had an offer for Leeds, but he wanted the best.'

'But London!' Emma exclaimed, as if it were the wilds of

Outer Mongolia instead of three hours away by train. 'I do hope he doesn't get himself murdered there, I mean, what with all them muggings and murders you hear about. Terrible murder last week, did you see it on t'news? A young lass strangled and chopped into little pieces. Little pieces, can you imagine?' and Emma shuddered in mock horror. 'Still, that's London for you! And drugs! Half the students in London are drug addicts, you know, I read about it in t'*Sun*. Hope your Dennis don't get in with the wrong crowd and go off the rails like some do, then he would never get to be a doctor, would he and all your pushing and going on at 'im will all come to nowt,' she added, pouring on the vitriol, drop by spiteful drop.

Susan's face crumpled and tears started to trickle down her face, although she tried hard to hold them back and deny Emma the pleasure of seeing how hurtful her words were. But even Emma, usually obliviously thick-skinned to the malice she spread, could hardly fail to see Susan's distress.

'Oh no, don't take on so, I'm sure it'll be alright, I were just worried, that's all, what wi' all the bad news these days. I blame the Common Market myself. I mean, it's not natural, is it, having to be friends with Germans and Frenchies? Anyhow, don't you take no notice of me, I'm just an old woman mithering away.'

Susan hurried off, but as she drove back towards the farmhouse, the impact of Emma's words echoed around her mind. Had she really driven Dennis to study medicine for her sake rather than his? He had never said he didn't want to be a doctor, but there again, he had never said that he did, either!

He had always been a quiet boy, introspective, not communicating very much, even more so since his dad died. The tractor had overturned on the steep slopes of the lower fields by Manstone Bottom, crushing him to a pulp. It had been Dennis who had found him. The farm had always been a shoestring operation, even more so after her husband's death and it had been so that he could break out of the vicious circle of poverty and endless hard work that she had encouraged – yes, that was the word, *encouraged* – Dennis to take up medicine. However, she was going to see Dennis soon and she could ask him about it then, just to set her mind at rest and give the lie to the insidious poison of Emma Arkwright's spiteful tongue.

All week, the vindictive words stayed with her, curdled like bile in her stomach and she was glad when she could finally take the twice-weekly bus into Leeds and board the London train and settle down for the journey.

Dennis looked pale and drawn as he walked into the room; the ruddy complexion from years on the farm seemed to have drained away, as if a wash of pallor had been brushed over him. Susan wanted to hug him to her, even though she knew she couldn't, not here.

'Hello, Mam,' he whispered, refusing to look her in the face.

She tried to speak but everything welled up and she burst into long-held-back tears. 'Dennis,' she croaked at last. 'Why?'

He appeared not to notice her distress. 'It's all your fault!' he said, his words sterile and lifeless. 'Goin' on at me all the time... going on about being a doctor. Never a thought about what I wanted, it was always what you wanted.' It was as though years of unspoken resentment were seeping out of him, a trickle leak in a dam wall that rapidly becomes a torrent.

'I were happy at home, working on the farm, with the animals and that. But no. "You're going to be a doctor, Dennis," you kept on saying. I only went along with it to shut you up.'

Susan shook her head and tried to close her ears to the hateful words. *It isn't true*, she told herself, *he's just saying this because he's lost and confused.*

'I only came to London to get away from you,' he continued, speaking more to himself than to Susan. 'If I'd been near home, you'd 'ave never stopped going about it. Makin' me come home at weekends to interrogate me. "How are your studies coming along, Dennis? When do you start treating people, Dennis? How long before you become a doctor, Dennis?" Couldn't stand it no more!'

Every word was like a stab to Susan's heart.

'I failed my exams, you know. I never am going to be a doctor. I couldn't face the thought of telling you and now you'll throw it all back at me, about wasting my opportunities and all the sacrifices you made for me.'

Susan wanted to rush from the room, but her legs seemed riveted to the chair as Dennis carried on remorselessly.

'I got drunk, didn't I? Never been as drunk as that before, had I? It was the night they told me I was being thrown out. This girl, she were laughing at me, saying I was a failure, a country bumpkin up from the sticks. Had my hands around her throat to make her shut up. Didn't mean no harm. But even after she were quiet, she were still laughing, so I cut her up. Chopped her up into little pieces. She weren't laughing at me then! And it's all your fault, Mam, All your fault...'

The train lurched into a bend at high speed and, with a jerk, Susan looked up, startled, totally disorientated, for one horrible moment unable to remember where she was. Outside the window, the countryside rushed past; through a small station, the pale faces of waiting passengers a pallid-streaked blur and then, with a swoosh that rocked her back from the window, the speeding express rocketed past an oncoming train. Shaken and confused, Susan looked around, trying to compose herself. She must have dozed off, but how on earth could she have been thinking such terrible things of Dennis? She felt ashamed and all the uncertainties raised by Emma Arkwright's wicked tongue rose again to the surface of her mind. For the rest of the journey, Susan could think of nothing else.

At King's Cross station, the throng of passengers surged and swirled around her as she studied the graffiti-splattered map of the London Underground, trying to make sense of it amid the scrawled obscenities, but for all she understood, it might as well have been a map of Mars.

With a sigh, she walked away from it and, anxiously mindful of how little money she had in her purse, climbed into a taxi and gave the address. Peering out of the taxi window, she hoped to see some reassuringly familiar sight, Big Ben or Nelson's Column or Buckingham Palace, but nothing; the taxi driver could be taking her anywhere and she would have no idea. She sat back in her seat, her heart beating loudly in trepidation.

Dennis sat down opposite her. He looked pale and drawn, the skin across his cheeks stretched and taut, the colour and texture of bleached parchment. He didn't say much, but then he never had. Afterwards, she went to see Dr Kincaird.

He shook hands limply and waved her to a chair. 'It must have been a tiring journey for you, Mrs Broadbent, coming all this way?' Susan could only nod, her mind incapable of small talk.

'How...how is Dennis getting along?' she asked hesitantly. 'He looks so tired.'

'I must be honest, Mrs Broadbent. Dennis is not so – how should I put it? – not so academically gifted as some of his fellow students and therefore he always had to work that much harder, just to keep pace, and the pressure has built up. If I might make an analogy, student life is very much like a pressure cooker and, as in a pressure cooker, there has to be a release valve. Which is why students tend to let rip during Rag Week, or on the rugger field. Dennis never seemed to be able to release that pressure. I also know that he felt the weight of your ambitions for him very heavily; indeed, I would even go so far as to say that it preyed on his mind. Ambition can be an extremely cruel taskmaster, Mrs Broadbent, especially when trying to live up to the expectations of others.'

'I never pushed him, Dr Kincaird. It was always his own choice.'

'I'm sure you believe that most sincerely, Mrs Broadbent, but nevertheless, there can be no doubt that Dennis felt greatly pressurised and so last week, when examinations loomed up, he had a minor nervous breakdown. You could say that his brain blew a fuse. I'm sorry, Mrs Broadbent, we'll keep him here for observation, but even if he recovers, I doubt he could ever take up his studies again. Quite simply, his brain would short out and he would suffer another breakdown. I'm afraid it's a case where extreme ambition brings about its own destruction.'

Susan could just imagine what Emma Arkwright was going to say about this.


'Excuse me, luv,' the taxi-driver said, and she jerked herself awake, blinking, her mind dislocated from reality. 'Here we are, Guys Hospital Medical School, that'll be £14.60, please.' She must have been dozing, suspended in that gelatinous semi-conscious state between sleep and wakefulness and once again she chided herself for the terrible visions she had had about Dennis.

Dennis looked as pallid as cold porridge, with deep-set black bags under his eyes. He gave her a tired smile that barely reached his eyes. 'Hello, Mum,' he said wearily.

'You look dreadful, Dennis. You've lost a lot of weight since you left home, and you don't look as you're getting enough sleep.'

He smiled ruefully. 'I think I've forgotten what sleep is, but I'll probably grab an hour or so later on. And how about you, Mum? And the farm and the village, still the same as ever?'

'Well, that cat Emma Arkwright had a go the other day. Saying that you never wanted to be a doctor, it was just me pushing you all the time?' She looked appealingly at Dennis, beseeching him with her eyes

'She always was a poisonous old ratbag, but I suppose she's right, really.'

Susan felt as though she had been slapped.

'I mean, I never really gave it much thought, did I? All my life you've been going on at me about being a doctor, so what I thought about it or what I felt about it never came into it. It was expected of me and so here I am.'

'I only did it for you, Dennis,' she mumbled, 'only for you.' She took a deep breath. 'You aren't going to give it, up are you?' she asked, visualising all the spiteful juice that Emma Arkwright would squeeze out of the orange of that particular situation.

'No, Mum, don't worry. I love it! Mind you, I didn't at first, in fact I hated it and I was almost ready to quit. And then, the most amazing thing happened. We had to attend a childbirth – only looking on, you understand? There were complications, the baby wasn't lying right, and it was touch and go whether it would survive. But it did and then to see that incredibly vibrant new life, it was amazing – miraculous – that's the only word to describe it, miraculous, and that's when I knew that I really did want to become a doctor. I decided there and then to specialise. I'm going to be an obstetrician.'

Susan Broadbent glowed. She just couldn't wait to see Emma Arkwright's face when she told her.

*Author's note. This is one of the very first short stories I ever wrote. It is now very dated but I still quite like it. I hope you did as well.*

# A LONG, LONG FINISH

My boss, who pretentiously likes to be called by his initials, DB, considers himself to be a wine buff. To the rest of humanity, he is a wine bore.

He is a world class bore, an Olympic Gold medal winner certainty for the Long Bore Event. Even his name is boring. Literally! Derek Boring, (hence DB). The rest of us call him Deadly Boring.

DB can pontificate about a glass of wine for hours and, like all deadly bores, considers himself to be erudite and entertaining, suffused with precious gems of oenology (the study of wine to you and me) that the rest of the world cannot wait to hear. He only ever drank vintage Chateau-bottled wines and (claimed) he would rather have gone without rather than sully his precious palate with anything from Australia, Chile, or the U.S., however good they might be. And, in his opinion, stated at great length, the only use for boxed wine was to flush out the drains when blocked.

Picture him at the restaurant table, entertaining some potential customers, glass in hand, broken-veined snout snuffling into the depths of his glass, commenting archly that to 'really appreciate the wine, the glassware should be nothing other than

Reidel Ouverture stem glass, Austrian you know, finest wine glasses in the world, expensive, naturally, but I never use anything else myself, of course'.

Sniff, sniff into the bowl of his Reidel Overture glass, waffling on about the 'second nose' being of prime importance.

A little sip, swirl it around the mouth as if he was going to gargle or maybe spit it out on the floor. 'Hmmm, excellent, excellent, Château Latrine du Publique, the 2015 vintage, of course.' Sip. Sip. Swirl. Swirl. 'Hmmm, excellent palate, creamy, silky texture, lots of heavy late season fruit, hints of rhubarb, blackcurrant Ribena, cherry, pomegranate and soy sauce, a *soupçon* of chocolate in there to give it depth.' Sniff, sniff. 'Yes, the nose and palate show great concentration and passion, masterful oak tannins, French oak of course, great varietals, very characteristic, yes, picked from the southern vineyard where the *ébourgeonnage* was the most effective, the late picking, probably...' sip, 'mid July, possibly on a Tuesday. Late afternoon, I'd say.' Sip. Sip. Swirl. 'Definitely Tuesday afternoon. Probably picked and trodden by Old Gaston Duturd, or possibly his son Phillippe. Sip. Sip. Swirl. Swirl. 'Hmm, no, definitely Old Gaston, I remember, he kept his socks on that year.'

Well, not quite, but you get the general idea.

The trouble was, in a moment of great foolishness, I had invited DB to dinner one evening. (It's not that I was sucking up to him for advancement, you understand, but it has seemed like a good idea at the time.) And I was sober.

My wife Suzie was horrified. 'How could you invite that odious bore to dinner? He's appalling, worse than novocaine. Deadly Boring! This is the most stupid idea you have ever had in your entire life and you have had some classics in your time, let me tell you.' Etc, etc.

But we were stuck with it. The problem was, what wine to serve? With the meagre pittance he paid me, there was no way I could afford to buy the bottles of Château Latour or de Rothschild that he would expect. Why had I been so foolish as to invite him?

Malcolm Berry, who owned the poshest restaurant in town, was an old friend of mine, we played for the same team in the Sunday Cricket league and so I went to see him, explained the dilemma and asked his advice

'What food will you be serving?' he asked.

'Well, Suzie's mother is Italian, so undoubtedly it will be something Italian and meaty. DB prefers meat dishes, something to get his juices working in greater harmony with his highly developed palate. Or something.'

'Italian and meat? In that case, Neil, it has to be an Amarone.'

'Amarone? Never heard of it, sounds like a cheap sickly perfume to me.'

'Amarone della Valpollicella Classico, to give it its full title, comes from the Veneto region of Northern Italy, the really top dog of Italian red wine.'

'DB only drinks French.'

'If he is as much a wine expert as he claims to be, he will know all about Amarone. A good vintage Amarone Allegrini, '04 or '08, will match anything France can produce.'

'Er, is it expensive?

'I'll show you.' And he showed me the catalogue and price list from his wine merchant. After I had picked myself up from the floor, I returned home with some bottles of Amarone (one for me and Suzie, two for DB).

With the antipasto misto, I served a Tasca D'Almerrita Regaleali Chardonnay, pricey but not all pretentious (unlike DB) and whilst DB did not actually spit it out in disgust, I could see he was not overly impressed.

For the main course, Suzie had done a sort of beef braised in red wine, the Italian name of which escapes me – she will kill me when she reads this, but whatever it was called, it was very good, a fillet of beef wrapped in prosciutto, stuffed with porcini and tomatoes, sprinkled with fresh rosemary and slow cooked in red wine, (a Barolo, not Amarone). With it she served baked polenta with four-cheese topping, insalata caprese (tomato and basil salad to you and me) and a green salad. Very good it was, too, makes me hungry all over again just thinking about it.

As Suzie served out the delicious beef fillet, I brought out the wine, 'I think you will like this one, DB, it's an Amarone,' He sniffed as if to show that it was most unlikely that he would like it and then I showed him the bottle.

'Good heavens, an '04 Amarone Monte Lodoletta Romano dal Forno. I must be paying you too much, Neil, this stuff sells at about £300 a bottle!' The look that Suzie gave me would have felled a lesser man, but I am made of sterner stuff and only suffered second degree burns.

I poured DB a glass of the Amarone Monte Lodoletta Romano dal Forno. He let it breathe for a minute or two then swirled it around in his glass (best local market, made in China), his snout quivering eagerly, like a truffle hound on the scent. He swirled the wine around the glass again, holding it to the light to check the rich ruby colour, to see how it clung to the side of the glass, the "fingers", before plunging his nose into the glass and inhaling deeply.

'Aah, ambrosia, the nectar of the gods.' I inwardly groaned; even I can spot tautology when I hear it

He truffled again, inhaling deeply. 'Excellent second nose, a heady bouquet, you can smell the raisins and sweet black fruit, classically Amarone.' Sniff, sniff. Finally a sip.

'Hmm, well-balanced, black cherry, thyme, a hint of plum maybe. Of course, if your palate is sufficiently discreet, as is mine, you can appreciate the subtle differences between the blended grapes, the Corvino blended with Rondinella and Molinara.' Sip. Sip. He closed his eyes and rolled the wine around his tongue and his oh-so-delicate palate. 'Evident oak, as you would expect, medium full to full body with excellent concentration. There is some rosemary in there, although not so evident as in the '97, of course.'

Suzie rolled her eyes at me and I could sense that possibly she might have something to say to me once DB had gone. 'The secret of Amarone, and not everybody knows this, is that the grapes are dried, *passito*, usually on straw matting for several months to give the wine that distinctive raisiny flavour, quite distinctive and giving those big tannins which are a major component of the finish. Should drink well for twelve to fifteen years. Long, long finish, fabulous nose, plum, oregano…' sip, '… definitely some black raspberry in there and the faintest aroma of tobacco, which of course you would expect.'

'Yes, of course,' responded Suzie tartly, but DB was too busy with his wine to notice.

DB waffled on in similar vein for the rest of the meal, repeating himself time and time again as he got into the second bottle. Myself, I thought the wine a bit sharp and vinegary, but there again, what do I know about wine? Finally he left, having drunk both bottles of the '04 Amarone Monte Lodoletta Romano dal Forno.

'How could you!' exploded Suzie, as soon as his taxi left. '£300 a bottle! Are you insane? Where are we going to find the best part of £1,000 to pay for it? For him, of all people! It was the most disastrous evening I have ever had, worse even than our honeymoon night when you passed out! I do not believe you sometimes, I really don't,' and so on and so on.

I let her have her say; I mean, what else could I do? It is perfectly true, '04 Amarone Monte Lodoletta Romano dal Forno does sell for around £300 a bottle. When she had exhausted her second or third tirade, I led her into the little workshop I have at the back of the garage. On the bench stood a funnel, two boxes of the cheapest, roughest Spanish red wine I could find, a box of Algerian white and some other empty bottles that Malcolm, my friend at the poshest restaurant in town, had given me. Just in case DB decides to come again.

# A KIND AND GENEROUS MAN

By the time I got there, my father's funeral had already begun.

Not wanting to disturb the proceedings, I just stood at the back of the crematorium chapel. My mother was at the front, dabbing her eyes with a pink tissue. My brother Decko sat beside her, his wife Pauline next to him and a couple of fidgeting kids next to her. There weren't many other mourners; none that I could recognise, anyway.

The priest was delivering the eulogy and I found it hard to connect his honeyed words of solace with the man I had known as my father. 'Edward Barclay will be much missed by his family; his widow Anthea, his sons, David–' (that's me) 'and Dennis–' (that's Decko) 'and grandchildren Wayne and Britney.' (The fidgeting rug-rats.)

'Ted, as he was more familiarly known,' the priest continued, 'was a kind and generous man, ever eager to lend a helping hand.' Aye, kind and generous to his mates when he was leaning over the bar at The Feather, I thought, and generous with his fists and belt to his wife and children when he got home,

'Aside from his family, Ted's other great passion was the Everleigh Cricket Club, and he spent many a happy hour at the club, watching the games and encouraging the youngsters coming through the club junior sides with his love for the sound of leather on willow.'

More like the sound of leather on flesh, I thought bitterly, and as far as his love for Everleigh Cricket Club went, it was just another excuse to lean over the bar 'til closing time. The priest, no doubt meaning well, droned on, but it was obvious he had never met Dad and his banal words of comfort were depressing rather than uplifting.

He came to the end and then announced that the next hymn would be *Abide with Me.* The congregation mumbled away at the words as the coffin slid slowly forward towards and then the red curtains swished across, hiding the coffin from view as it continued on its final journey to the incinerator.

I thought back to the last time I had seen him.

I was eighteen at the time and still living at home. I worked at the local bookshop, but I had plans to study, maybe go on to college, become a teacher.

It was late, almost midnight, and Decko and I were in bed. We shared the back bedroom where we each had a single bed. There was a wardrobe and a five-drawer chest of drawers and a ladder-backed chair. Dad had been down the pub as usual and came back in a foul temper – as usual. I heard shouts, a stifled scream from Mum and then the sounds of him stamping up the stairs. Decko, who was thirteen at the time, gave me a haunted look and then hid under the bedclothes.

Dad flung open the bedroom door and lurched across to my bed, leaning over me to shout, his breath foul with drink and tobacco, his teeth as yellow as rancid butter. He was shouting that I had moved some papers and letters; he was paranoid about anybody touching his possessions and would frequently accuse us of moving them about – we never did – wouldn't dare – but once he had got it into his sodden brain that me or Mum had moved something, we knew a beating was coming. For him, any excuse would do.

I saw his belt in his hand. He would leather me first and then

Mum would get some. Decko usually escaped with a slap or two.

'Get up, you little bastard,' he hissed, as he slashed at me through the bedclothes, 'I'll teach you!'

He slashed again and a sudden, vivid red anger blazed through me like lava and I leapt out of bed with the absolute realisation that I was now bigger than he and did not have to take this any longer. He must have seen the look on my face, and he backed away, but all the years of hate and humiliation at his hands came flooding through me in a heated torrent. I snatched the belt from his hands and began to lay about him, across his back, his arms, legs, face, anywhere; all those years, all those beatings.

For how long I flailed at him, I don't know. He was a crumpled heap on the floor, his hands about his head as I stood over him, panting from my exertions. I flung the belt aside and I knew that I had to get out. I quickly dressed and then ran to the other bedroom and grabbed a suitcase from the top of his wardrobe and began to stuff my other clothes in. In my haste, I pulled one of the drawers completely out, spilling the contents all across the floor.

Dad lay there unmoving while my mother stood at the bedroom door, sobbing quietly, holding her side where he had punched her. She looked at me in mute desperation, tears of pain and heartache trickling down her face as she watched me pack. She knew – as did I – that my leaving would change nothing. Tomorrow would be the same and he would take it out on her even more.

'Where will you go?' she asked.

'I'll phone, tell you where I am,' I said.

'What about work, David?'

'Tell them I've left. Get them to send my money and P45 on.'

'Can't you stay, sort this out?'

'I can't, Mum. I just can't stay under the same roof as him anymore.'

'Aye, but the rest of us have to.'

'You don't have to, Mum. Leave him, he doesn't deserve you.'

She gave a sad smile. '"For better or worse," I vowed,' she said. '"Til death do us part". It still means something, you know, David.'

'If he hurts you again…'

She smiled that sad smile again – we both knew that they were hollow words.

'Stay till the morning at least,' she said.

'I can't. If I stay here a minute longer, I'll end up killing him.'

I picked up my suitcase, gave her quick peck on the cheek, said goodbye to Decko and ran down the stairs and out into the night.

That was the last time I ever saw him.


The service had come to an end. I walked down to see my mother. I gave her a hug. 'Thank you for coming, David,' she whispered through her sobs. I could feel her chill tears through my shirt. 'I didn't know whether you would be able to.'

'I had to come, didn't I?'

'He asked for you at the end, you know, David. At the end, when he knew. He never stopped – never stopped loving you, despite everything.'

I didn't know what to say, words would have been so trite, so I just gave her another tight squeeze, but we are not much given to public shows of affection in our family and we quickly broke apart.

'Hello, Decko,' I said, turning to my brother. He scowled at the use of his childhood nickname.

'Decko?' queried his wife Pauline and he gave her such a brutal look that I knew – knew without doubt – that it was like father, like son; Decko was a bully and wife-beater.

I still had my hand held out and reluctantly he took it and we shook hands. I could see the resentment in his face and could not at first understand and then the realisation hit me. I had deserted him, left him to face the wrath of Dad on his own and he hated me for it. I gave the children, my nephew and niece, a nod; they looked at me as though I had come from another planet and then began whispering behind their hands.

We started to file out of the chapel, Decko importantly taking up station alongside Mum and taking her arm, Pauline to the other side, the kids in tow and I was left to follow on like a road-sweeper after the dust cart. Music was softly playing in the background; I couldn't work out the tune at first and then realised it was the theme from *The Magnificent Seven*, just about the only piece of music Dad had liked. Mum must have requested it.

By the door, the priest, who didn't look old enough to shave, shook hands with the departing mourners – not that I really qualified as a mourner – and the little gaggle of relatives and friends worked their way along the chapel colonnade to look at the floral tributes. There weren't very many of them.

The undertaker then collected all the cards from the flowers and gravely presented them to Mum. She looked at them once more before putting them into her handbag. The pink tissue she had used to wipe her eyes fluttered out of her sleeve, where she had tucked it during the service. Nobody seemed inclined to pick it up.

I felt a tug on my left wrist. Mr Hansen looked at his watch. 'Time to go, David,' he said. I gave Mum a last hug, nodded to Decko and the kids and walked along with Hansen back to the waiting car; my left wrist handcuffed to his right.

I'm serving a life sentence in Wakefield Gaol for a double murder committed during a robbery. What is it they say? "Violence begets violence" and "the sins of the fathers are visited on the sons."

I didn't bother to look back as we drove away.

# MY NAME IS STEVIE

750 words, he said. Give me your life story in 750 words.

I am an alcoholic in rehab and so this life story exercise is part of the therapy. How I got to where I was, the dark places I'd been, down in the gutter and worse, much worse, the story to be discussed with all the others in the group.

So here goes: I was born in Sheffield, my dad was a solicitor and a drunkard, Mum just a drunk. When they weren't drinking, they argued and when they weren't arguing, they drank. Never any time for me. I think I came as a surprise, a nasty surprise, to them.

When I was nine, my uncle Kevin started to abuse me – abuse me sexually. I told my mother, but she wouldn't have it, Kevin being her brother and Dad just took his belt to me for telling lies and so the abuse continued. One day when I was about twelve, I tried to run away, stole money from Mum's purse and made my way to the station where I asked for a ticket to London, but the ticket clerk realised I was a runaway and called the police. I got another beating from my dad for my trouble.

Social services had got involved, but they didn't really give a toss, being more concerned in covering their own backsides.

Anyway, my dad said I was an incorrigible liar and they took his word over mine, him being a solicitor and all that.

I was a bright kid, but my schooling went to rat-shit and I started drinking. There was always drink about the house and so I'd take a sip here, a swig there.

I was fourteen when I finally ran away to London. I was wandering around St Pancras, not knowing what to do next, when this bloke came up to me. 'Hi, kid, you look hungry, fancy a burger?' he said. After the burger, he said he ran a karate school: would I like to learn some karate, help me take care of myself on the streets? He took me to this house. There were other kids there, but they weren't doing no karate. The bloke was not the one who raped me, but others did, plenty of them.

Once you've been raped, they've got you, see; they make you too ashamed to tell anybody. They ply you with drink and drugs to keep you compliant and sell you out to the paedos. It's a gang-run thing, with important people involved, judges, politicians, ministers and the like, top coppers paid to look away. Then, if you are a boy, once you get to seventeen or thereabouts, you're too old for the paedos and so I was kicked out, but not before I got a real beating to warn me to keep quiet. Girls, of course are kept, or else sold on to the Albanian-run brothels.

There I was, out on the streets, no clue what to do, living rough, selling myself to buy booze. Cheap vodka and cider mixed, that's the quickest way to get hammered. Once, I met this Aussie bloke, Wayne or Shane, who got me onto metho; that's methylated spirits, Brasso and melted-down boot polish. A hell of a kick but rat-shit for the guts. I spent a couple of weeks in a squat, but the others didn't much like what I did, selling myself, and kicked me out, afraid of AIDS, so I was out on the streets again.

There was a girl, Crystal she called herself, but I don't think it was her real name. She was an addict, heroin, selling herself to pay for her habit. We sort of got together and she got pregnant, don't know how, alkies like me normally have problems down there. It was a girl, the baby. Crystal called her Sancha, don't know why. She struggled to live at first, Sancha, because of the heroin in her system, but of course she got took into care and came through. Then Crystal died, an overdose; gave me a real jolt, that did and that's when I decided I had to clean myself up else I was going the same way. Besides, I want Sancha to know who her dad is. OK, I know I'll never be allowed to have her, but it would be something just to see her, something to get clean for. Maybe get some learning, college, get a proper job.

So here I am in rehab. I've relapsed twice before, but this time, third time lucky, I'll stick it for sure.

My name is Stevie and I'm an alcoholic.

# AND IN THE SHIMMERING LIGHT
# OF DAWN

*Stalag 23*
*Germany*
*December 22, 1917*

*My dearest darling girl,*

*As you can see from the above, I am now a prisoner of the Hun.*

*We went over the top, I can't tell you where, but me and Nobby Tune
and Jim Collins and couple of the other lads got stranded behind the
lines. I'm sorry to say that they didn't make it, but I was captured after
being wounded in the knee but nothing really to worry about. We are
cheerful enough here although it is awful cold, the huts we live in are
made from thin planks, not too much to keep out the chilly winds,
The food is not much, the sausages seem to be made from sawdust and I
dare not speculate what goes into the soup and stews, but we are not
mistreated.
We keep our chins up and you must do the same, my love. It won't be
long now till I am home, and we can wed.*

*Well my dearest, this is the only piece of paper I have and so I must finish. Give my best regards to your mother.*

*As ever,*
*Your loving Arthur.*
*XXX*

*Ps Hope to hear from you soon with your darling letters.*

Pvt. Arthur Hanbury sealed the envelope and carefully wrote the address:

*Miss Ada Pierce*
*27, Helena Street*
*Millwall*
*London*

As he did so, Arthur could visualise the tiny terraced house, just off the East India Dock Road, where his Ada lived; the blue front door, the spotless white net curtains and the whitewashed front step. He missed her enormously and wished that they had been able to marry during his last furlough, but her mother had been dead set against it, thinking Arthur not good enough for Ada; quite where she got her airs and graces from Lord only knows.

*The Daily Sketch*
*January 13th, 1918*

*TERROR ZEPPELIN RAID OVER LONDON DOCKS*
*MANY CASUALTIES.*

*Germany yesterday launched Zeppelin terror raids over London dock-lands, many civilians casualties have been reported as the Hun bombed residential streets in Poplar and Millwall ....*

*Stalag 23*
*February 12, 1918*

*My dearest Ada,*
*I have not heard from you of late, I can only hope that your eagerly awaited letters have been delayed. I am well...*

*Stalag 23*
*April 29, 1918*

*My dearest Ada,*
*Still no word from you and I begin to worry. I cannot write as regular as I would like as paper is in very short supply. I can only imagine that a similar shortage prevents you from writing*
*My wounded knee is not too clever but not to worry ...*

*Stalag 23*
*June 26, 1918*

*My dear Ada,*
*It is now 6 months or more since I last heard from you. Here in the prison camp I have nothing else to occupy my mind and I am going crazy, thinking all manner of thoughts about you. Have you given your affections to another? If so, please tell me, I will try to understand ...*

*Stalag 23*
*September 12th, 1918.*

*Dear Ada,*
*This is the last time I will write ...*

The war ended on 11th November 1918, but it was some weeks before Arthur could be repatriated to England. His wounded knee gave him a great deal of trouble and he spent four anxious and frustrated weeks at a military hospital in France from where, on clear days, he could see the coast of England, so tantalisingly close – so very far away. He thought of Ada every day and even though he knew she had now abandoned him for another, he was determined to find her and hear it from her own lips. Only then would he be able to put her out of his mind.

Arthur caught the 12.25 train from Fenchurch Street Station. As the train trundled through the East End streets towards Ada's house, he was surprised at the amount of bomb damage; whole streets seem to have been flattened and he felt a churning worm of anxiety gnawing at his stomach as he got off the train at Poplar Station and crossed the East India Dock Road and into Helena Street.

Most of the street had completely vanished; all that remained were broken walls and shattered brickwork. Only part of one wall remained of Ada's house. Arthur could see the blue and yellow flowered wallpaper that her mother had been so proud of, now peeling and rain-stained; the rest of the house was just a large bomb crater, half filled with water in which floated a bloated dead cat.

Now Arthur knew why Ada had never replied to his letters.

By the edge of the crater he muttered a prayer and apologised to Ada for ever having doubted her.

Wiping away his tears, he made his way back to the station.

Life has to go on...

Arthur found a job as a guard on the railways. He never married and lived by himself in rooms over a tobacconist shop in Holloway, North London. He still thought of Ada every day.

When war broke out in 1939, Arthur tried to enlist, but was rejected on account of his crippled knee. He consoled himself by reasoning that the efficient running of the railways was vital to the war effort – and at least he was in some kind of uniform.

The air raid had been going on for some time and Arthur's train was held up by bomb damage to the line up ahead. Stiffly, he climbed down from the guards van, trying to peer up the line to see what the hold-up was. Then air-raid sirens began to wail again as a second wave of bombers came over. This time the bombing was closer, and the train rocked and shivered as a stick of bombs fell close by, the dark night-sky seared with explosions and the criss-crossing shafts of searchlight beams.

Arthur knew he ought to get to a shelter, even though he hated to leave his post. As he deliberated, a cluster of bombs ripped open the front of the train and he was flung aside by the force of the blast. More bombs were falling. He crawled up over the embankment by the bridge and out into the street. Many of the houses were ablaze.

'You should be in the shelters, mate,' a passing air raid warden called. 'There's some Anderson shelters just behind here, in these back gardens, get yourself in there sharpish.'

The shrieking whistle of falling bombs followed as Arthur hurried into the garden, finding his way to a corrugated iron shelter by the light from the burning buildings.

Frightened faces of children peered at him as he hobbled into the shelter, finding space at the end of the bench.

'Sorry to just drop in like this,' he said, having to shout over the noise, 'only the whole street has gone up and the warden sent me in here. Hope you don't mind.'

'Course not, ducks, we're a right mixed bunch in here anyways, full of waifs and strays,' answered a cheery woman from the depths of the shelter.

'Did you say the whole street has gone up?' another woman asked.

''Fraid so'

'Oh Lord, this is the second time I've been bombed out of house and home,' the unseen voice sobbed and as she spoke, the hairs on the back of Arthur's neck rose and he felt a shiver running through his body like an electric shock.

'Ada?' he asked hesitantly, 'Ada, is that you?' scarcely able to hear his own words for the pounding of his heart and the rush of blood in his ears. 'Ada Pierce?'

'Who's that? I've not been called Ada Pierce for fifteen year or more!'

Arthur felt his heart soar. It was his Ada, after all these years of thinking her dead in the ruins of her house. 'It's me, Arthur, Arthur Hanbury.'

'Is this some sort of cruel joke? Arthur Hanbury is dead. He died in France in 1917.'

'No, it's me, Ada. I thought you was dead, I went to the house and everything, they told me everyone in the house had died'

'The War Office told me you had died, you and all your platoon.'

'Didn't you never get my letters?'

'No. Like I said, they said you was dead and the house in Helena Street gone, Mum and Dad and brother Jack, Oh, Arthur,' she sobbed, 'is it you, is it truly you?'

'Yes, my girl, it's me. Truly.'

'Give me your hand, hold me Arthur.' Arthur reached out across the smoky darkness, feeling for the hands of his only love.

He brushed against her hand as she leaned towards him, searched again, found her hand and held it tight, squeezing himself closer to hold it to his heart. He pressed her hand to his lips, feeling grit and dirt on her fingers but caring not.

''Ere, ducks,' the woman next to him said, 'come in ere,' and she moved aside to let Arthur deeper into the shelter, closer to his Ada. Arthur gently pulled Ada towards him, feeling for her face, tracing her lips with his fingers, wiping away the tears which rolled down her face.

'Oh Ada, my darling girl,' he said as she came into his arms, her tears cold on his chest.

'Arthur. Arthur,' Ada whispered, over and over.

They clung together, sobbing gently.

Arthur had to ask. 'You've said you've not been called Ada Pierce for fifteen years. Does that mean you're wed? Wed to another?' It would be too cruel to have found her after all these years, only for her to be married to someone else.

Ada sobbed deeply, clinging to him ever more tightly and Arthur feared her answer.

'I'm a widow, Arthur. I did marry, I married Billy Shears, he was in the Merchant Navy, but he went down with his ship last year.'

'Oh, Ada, I'm so sorry'

He felt her shaking her head. 'No, no, it's all in the past' She paused for the longest seconds. 'Did you ever marry?' she asked hesitantly.

'Me? No! There was only ever you for me.'

'I'm so sorry I didn't wait for you, Arthur, but…'

Arthur held her even tighter. 'I know we need time to get to know each other again, but Ada Pierce, Ada Shears, whatever, will you marry me?'

'Oh yes, Arthur. Oh yes, I will!'

Somebody in the shelter started clapping; then everybody joined in clapping and crying, relieving their fears and terrors, glad that some little good had come from the devastation wrought upon them from the skies.

The all-clear sounded and in the shimmering light of dawn, Arthur and Ada walked out from the shelter and through the destruction to start their long-delayed new lives together.

# BILLY O'SHAUNESSY'S LAST STAND
## A SMALL YORKSHIRE TOWN, SUMMER 1955.

When Inspector Christopher Yarrow arrived at the police station that morning, he parked his car and, as he did most mornings, stopped to chat with the night duty Sergeant, Sgt. Dave Armitage, whom Yarrow had known for years. Many a time they had been for a pint in The Dog and Bacon, or Armitage's local, The Castle on Digby Road.

Although Armitage seemed ageless, he was actually nearing his retirement and dreaded it more and more with every passing day. 'What am I goin' to do, Chris?' he often asked. 'I mean, I don't play golf, a game for ponces and Chief Constables that is. I hate the bloody garden, no way I'm goin' to be growin' prize leeks like Arthur Millward did when 'e retired and how long did he last before he keeled over, eh? I'm fed up wi' watchin' the Rovers lose every bloody week, the old woman's already grum- blin' about me goin' to be under her feet all day... what the bloody 'ell am I goin' to do? I tell yer what I'll be bloody doin'. I'll be pushing up the daisies inside a month, died of boredom if I haven't strangled her first. She should be the landlady at The Nag's Head, the tongue on 'er!'

That Dave Armitage was utterly devoted to his Edith never

GILES EKINS

stopped him complaining endlessly about her and Yarrow usually let it wash over him with an indulgent smile on his face.

The same theme with slight variations and cadences came up virtually every time Yarrow spoke to Armitage, but he still enjoyed talking to him, remembering fondly that when he first joined the force Armitage had looked out for him, as he did all new green coppers.

'Morning, Dave, anything on? Seems a bit quiet.'

'Nah, not a lot, quiet night last night, the only trade I've got is Billy Shaunessy, sleepin' it off in Number 2.'

'Billy Shaunessy... you mean Billy O'Shaunessy?'

'Nope, Billy Shaunessy, says 'e' lost the O somewhere and don't know where to find it, so it's Billy Shaunessy without an O from now on. Leastwise 'til he finds his O again.'

'What's he in for, D & D as usual?'

'Yeah, Drunk and Disorderly as per usual and, just for a change, Indecent Exposure.'

'What? That doesn't sound like Billy!'

'That's what I would say, but an old biddy complained that she was walking her dog in Gallipoli Park when Billy exposed himself to her.'

'That's where Billy sleeps out most nights, Gallipoli Park, under that big willow by the duck pond.'

'Aye, well that where she said it 'appened, right there.'

'What else did she say? You're sure it was Billy?'

'She said she knows Billy, everybody in town knows Billy, One-Legged Billy. She sniffed a lot and said it was disgusting and why didn't the police do summat about it, letting vagrants loose in council property... and more of the same, proper old battle-axe. I says as far as I know, parks is for everyone and last time I looked this was a free country an' that's what we fought a war for, an' she says I'm a disgrace to me uniform an' that she's the wife of Councillor Ferguson, an' that 'e's a close friend of the Chief Constable and she's goin' to report me. Scared me down to me boots, she did, I bloody well don't think. Worse than my missus she was and that's sayin' summat, I can tell thee. Any'ow, I asked for details, like did he have an erection when he exposed himself, that sort of thing – I mean, flashers do it with a hard-on, don't they?'

'I'll take your word on that, Dave,' Yarrow answered dryly.

'You'd 'ave thought I'd asked her to hold a dog turd, the way she looked at me when I asked 'er that. The face on her! But eventually she did sort of say yes, he did have that... what it was you said.'

'It still doesn't sound right. Look, Dave, I've known Billy Shaunessy, with or without an O, for as long as I've been in this nick and you a good deal longer, I dare say. Look, he did his bit in the war and lost a leg for his troubles and OK, now he's a drunk, a derelict vagrant who stinks like a decomposing polecat most of the time, but I'd bet my pension that he's basically harmless, he's never been in any sort of trouble before apart from D & D. I just can't see it, Dave.'

'Me neither, but she is adamant. And as she's the wife of Councillor Maurice Ferguson, poor bastard, as she never left off telling me, I dare say the magistrates'll tek her word rather than his.'

'What does Billy say about all this?'

'Not a lot, says he was taking a piss, didn't see her or her dog 'til she started on yellin' and screamin' fit to bust her corsets.'

'I'll go and have a word, see if I can make some sense out of it.'

'Aye, right, I'll bring him along. Grab a cuppa and I'll put him in the interview room. Mind you, we'll have to disinfect and delouse it after, 'e's real dead ripe today.'

Yarrow collected his tea from the canteen and one for Billy (six sugars, alcoholics just crave sugar) and stepped into the interview room.

The stench hit him like an open sewer – no, worse than that, a thick, choking effluvia of long unwashed body, rank urine, weeks' old shit, this morning's shit, dog shit, cat piss, vomit, sweat, and Lord alone knew what else. Yarrow had to hold his hand to his mouth, hardly daring to breath, taking only shallow breaths until his nose got used to the rawness of the stink.

'Morning, Billy, got yourself in a spot of bother again. Cuppa tea for you here.'

'Oh! Oh, 'tis you, Mr Yarrow, and how are you dis foin mornin?' Billy's Irish lilt was undiminished even though he had lived in and around the town for as long as most people could remember.

'Just fine, Billy. Now, you just drink up your tea and we'll have us a little chat, see if we can sort out what happened.'

Billy held his cup in both hands to stop the shaking; even so, the lip of the cup rattled against what remained of his teeth. 'T'ank youse, Mr Yarrow, a body needed that, but if you'd be so kind, a bit more sugar the next time, not that Oi'm ungrateful, like, but a body does crave the sweetness.'

Yarrow waited until Billy had finished drinking and laid down his cup. Yarrow took out his cigarettes, lit one for himself and passed another over to Billy, tossing him the box of matches as he didn't wish to get too close by lighting it for him, since his breath would stop a herd of rampaging warthogs. Even as Billy lit up, a dribble of saliva drooled onto the table top and Yarrow almost expected the varnish to bubble and shrivel as if attacked by acid.

'God bless, you, Mr Yarrow,' said Billy, drawing in the smoke with deep satisfaction, his normal smoke being roll-ups made with tobacco collected from dog-ends he found in the street or in dustbins.

'So tell me, Billy, last evening, Mrs Ferguson?'

'Dat lying old cow!'

'Is she lying, Billy? Mrs Ferguson claimed you exposed yourself to her and that you had an erection. That's indecent exposure, you could go down for that, you know.'

'Me, with a stiffie? Don't you know notting, Mr Yarrow? I'm a meths drinker. OK, a bit of sweet Cyprus sherry when I've a coin or two when the Disability comes in, but for me, it's mostly meths, sometimes boiled down with Brasso and boot polish. Now dat stuff, meths, Brasso and boot polish, dat'll give you'se a hell of a jolt right enough, but it doesn't just do for your liver, you know, it does for your dick and bollocks. Jaysus, I haven't had a stiffie since 1942 when I was in Egypt with the Army. Me and some mates went to see this exotic dancer as she called herself, Port Said it was. Jaysus, the things she did with that bottle and that snake, you wouldn't believe it. Lucky old snake, I say. And that was the last time me old fella looked at the ceilin' rather than staring at the floor. Me wit' a stiffie? the old biddy's dreaming. Else hopin'!'

'Is that the truth, Billy, you can swear that in court?'

'Aye, to be sure, and any doc who's dealt with alkies can swear to the same, so they can. The trut' is, I was taking a piss behind the tree, needed it real bad, then suddenly I hears this screamin' and yellin' fit to wake the Holy Saints in their Heaven and bugger me, there the old bitch is standin,' yellin' and pointing. Jesus, made me jump six foot in the air, pissed myself all down me leg, so I did, then see if she don't set the dog on me, one of them shitty little yappy things, snappin' at my ankles like a demented hairbrush. No, I admit to taking a piss behind the tree, but I didn't see her an', to be sure, if I was going to flash a stiffie around, it wouldn't be to a dried-up, prune-faced old bag like dat, dat's for sure.'

'OK, Billy, I believe you and I'll talk to the desk sergeant and get you released, maybe with a caution not to urinate in public.'

'Thank you, Mr Yarrow. S'appreciated, so it is. So's I can get back down to the park. I had to leave all me stuff, all me worldly goods and chattels and I'm dead bothered that some thieving bastard'll have it away.'

Yarrow smiled. He knew that Billy's worldly goods and chattels consisted of an old army kitbag, two rancid blankets, a rubberized groundsheet, a meths camping cooker, an old saucepan, a tin plate and mug, knife, spoon, a battered *Complete*

*Works of William Shakespeare* and old shopping bags he filled when scavenging around rubbish bins for scraps of food, fag ends and anything else he found useful. And, in a battered, leather-clad box the size of the packet of Players, a Military Medal, won by Billy in North Africa in the action that had cost him his leg.

Billy took another deep drag on his Players and broke out into a fierce, lung-ripping coughing spasm, the tears streaming down his face as he hacked and sputtered, turning deathly white. Yarrow could hear the racking wheeze in Billy's lungs. The old derelict looked pale and ill and trembling, sick to the core. Yarrow knew that most rough-sleeping drunks did not die from the effects of excessive alcohol, it was the general deterioration of health occasioned by poor food, lack of hygiene and sleeping rough in inclement weather; pneumonia killed far more drunks than the grog ever did.

'Billy, why do you sleep rough all the time? Why not go down to the Sally, the Salvation Army on Dreadnought Street? You'll get a bed, and a bath and God knows you could do with one. And they'll check you out medically. You don't sound too good to me.'

'Me? At the Sally, havin' to go to Chapel on Sunday and join in them services and sing them tambourine hymns, just to get a bed? Now, Mr Yarrow, I was raised as a good Catholic boy, so I was, and if Father Murphy at St Mary's knew I'd been to the Sally Army, he'd excommunicate me, so he would.'

Yarrow knew it was hopeless to argue with Billy that the Sally did not proselytize or try to convert; instead, he took out his wallet from his inside jacket pocket and handed Billy a ten bob note. 'Get down to the Machin Street Baths then. And see a doctor.'

'Bless you, Mr Yarrow, 'tis a saint you are, I'll be straight down the baths as soon as I collect my stuff.' But Yarrow could see the yearning in Billy's eyes and knew the money would go on drink just as soon as the off-licence opened. For a drunk, alcohol took far greater precedence than bodily hygiene or even his own health.

'Sure thing, Billy. Just wait here a minute and we'll get you out of here as soon as we can.'

Leaving the almost full packet of twenty Players and the box of Bryant and Mays, Yarrow stepped out of the interview room and, resisting the urge to run outside and let the wind blow away some of the stink, he made his way over to Armitage at the front desk, who pointedly held his nose as Yarrow approached.

'I believe him, Dave. Apparently alkies can't raise an erection. The grog gets into their works and they can't… rise to the occasion, shall we say?'

Dave Armitage broke into a broad smile and waited his moment like a good comedian, for whom timing is all. After a long, pregnant silence, he said, deadpan: 'So what you're saying is… that it won't stand up in court!'

# SUNSET OVER THE GRAND CANYON

What I did on my holidays? Well, actually, I didn't do a lot. Couldn't do a lot.

Whilst my friends were out and about, doing things, going places, I was confined to a wheelchair following a motorbike accident. I had been riding pillion behind my elder brother Carl on his Kawasaki, when he lost control going through a slippery slick of cow-dung on a rain-wet country road. We both came off the bike. Carl was uninjured apart from a few scrapes and grazes, but I broke my left leg in two places and cracked my patella when I careered knee-first into a dry-stone wall. That'll bring tears to your eyes, I can tell you.

After leaving hospital, Mum turned the dining room into a bedroom for me as it was difficult for me to climb up and down the stairs with my leg in plaster. She set up a bed and I had my computer, Play-station, books and a portable television, but I quickly got bored with them. I wheeled myself around the garden and the house, growing increasingly frustrated and my skin itched unbearably under the plaster which encased my leg from thigh to shin and I had to use a chopstick to scratch at the bits it could reach

Bill and Maxie, my two best mates, came round to see me at

first. They signed my cast but then they soon got bored with me being bored. Besides, Maxie was going to Sardinia with his parents and Bill was going off camping and rock-climbing with Mickey Paling and Doug Brooks in Wales. I should have been going with them, we'd been planning it since Easter. Secretly, I hoped it would rain on them all the time.

But no. The sun shone, the birds sang, and all my friends had gone off somewhere for their holidays and I was stuck at home in a wheelchair and although Mum and Dad and Carl (feeling guilty) did take me out occasionally, the inactivity and confinement was suffocating. Boredom drove me down like a wedge driven into my skull.

'Why don't you do a jigsaw?' my mother asked helpfully. 'You always used to enjoy doing jigsaws when Auntie Marie came to stay.'

'Nah, that was yonks ago, when I was a kid. Jigsaws are boring, everything is boring. Life is boring,' I answered snappily, feeling very sorry for myself.

'There's no need to take it out on me, my lad, I was only offering suggestions to try and think of things to do.'

'Yeah, yeah, I know, I'm sorry,' and, more to make up to her for being snappy than any real desire to actually do a jigsaw, I said, 'OK, I'll try a jigsaw but not any of the ones we've already got. Can you get me a new one, 'bout a thousand pieces? An action film one, not soppy flowers or thatched cottages?'

'I'll see what they've got when I go into town.'

The Grand Canyon at Sunset was hardly what I had in mind, but Mum said there wasn't much choice, and this did have a Red Indian in it; it was either this one or the Alps, Ayers Rock, a painting of some horses in a field, or Pink Barbie. I think I would have preferred the Barbie.

I left the jigsaw in the box for a couple of days to let her know what I thought of it, but I realised I was being petty, as she had done the best she could, and it wasn't her fault that Jimson's Toy Shop, the only one in town, had such a poor selection.

It was actually a very nice picture, a painting of the Grand Canyon at sunset. The azure sky was streaked with shards of many shades of orange and crimson, wine and deepening purple; bright bursts of colour from the setting sun sent shafts of gold, orange and vermillion spinning into the layered depths and rich earth hues of the canyon, where reds and oranges and crimson darkened into shadowed strata of violet and purple and cobalt blues, the deepest shadows blackening with intensity. Sunlight glittered from the river far below, glinting and shimmering like a silver-gold thread running through a tapestry.

On a high promontory which projected over the canyon like the prow of a ship, there stood a lone Indian facing the setting sun. He was bare-chested, arms outstretched as though to bid farewell to the departing day. His head was tilted back, the rays of the dying sun casting red-orange highlights onto his bronzed face. From his head there trailed a war-bonnet, a full eagle-feather headdress that flowed down his back and legs almost to the ground. He was magnificent, so perfect in composition, placed – not in the centre of the picture – but to the right of centre, in the heart of the Golden Mean, that perfection of proportion created by the Old Masters that irresistibly draws in the eye to the soul of the painting.

An eagle, wings outspread, soared above the canyon, riding the thermals as the undisputed master of the skies.

The proud-standing Indian was only a small figure in the vastness of the great landscape, as if to illustrate how insignificant man is, compared to the grandeur of nature, but even so, it was that tiny, sun-drenched figure that drew you into the picture.

I decided I was going to enjoy doing the jigsaw after all.

I opened the box and tore open the polythene and poured the pieces, all 1000 of them, across the dining table. According to the box, the finished size would be 29' x 22', approximately 75cm x 56cm; from my wheelchair, I would just about be able to reach far enough over the table to get to the furthermost limits.

I separated out all the edge pieces and put all the other pieces back in the box for now. Setting up the right hand corner, I slowly put together the outer frame. The strip across the top of the puzzle was the most difficult since the sky was a brilliant uniform cerulean blue. Only towards the upper left-hand corner did the shards of setting sun splice into the clean azure.

Once I had finished the outer edges, I emptied all the other pieces onto the table and sorted them all out, turning them face-up. I had to spread them around the room; there wasn't enough space on the table for all the pieces to be within reach. Pieces were spread out over the sideboard as well.

The silver line of the river was easy to pick out and I soon had that snaking across from the lower left side.

Around the river line, I was soon able to build up the base of the canyon, for here the colours were deeper and shaded, purple and dark violet and deepest sapphire merging into the darkness of shadowcast.

The shadows and depths of the ravine eased out into the sunlight, slowly climbing the face of the canyon walls. Often as not, I stood up now, hobbling and hopping around the table and across to the sideboard to track down another piece.

I kept on looking for the Indian chief. It should have been an easy piece to find, but, hunt as I could, I could not locate him. I reasoned that perhaps he was on a number of pieces, which would make him more difficult to trace.

The eagle also took shape and I was able to make the connection from him to the rim of the canyon. Working around the eagle, I finished the sunset-streaked sky.

It would be true to say I became obsessed with the jigsaw. I would set myself goals; ten pieces fitted before I had breakfast, thirty pieces in the morning, another thirty in the afternoon – not as easy as you might think.

The sun-soaked promontory took shape, but still I could not find the pieces for him, the magnificent, proud-standing Chief.

The entire canyon was now in place and I began to feel

uneasy. There did not seem to be enough pieces left to complete the puzzle.

And then there were no more pieces left to place and one piece, just one piece, was missing – the chief! There was a bit of his headdress, an outstretched arm, but that was it.

I searched under the table, under the sideboard, I even got Carl to pull the sideboard out to make sure the piece hadn't fallen down behind – but no, it wasn't there.

I felt deflated and betrayed. All that effort, for nothing! The puzzle was ruined, the gap where the missing piece should be shouted out like an insult.

I rang Jimson's to complain, to see if they had another puzzle in stock, but they said no – they were not really interested, to be honest – all they could say was write to the manufacturer to complain. As the puzzle was made in Taiwan, I didn't hold up much hope of that.

Absurdly furious, I pulled the puzzle apart and threw the pieces into the box and flung the box into the waste bin in the kitchen and refused to let anybody take it out.

Three days after I had "finished" the puzzle, I went back to the hospital to have my cast cut off. The nurse sawed down both sides and peeled the cast apart.

And out fell the missing piece!

# UNDERNEATH THE CLOCK TOWER

'Underneath the Clock Tower? At eight? That'll be brilliant, just brilliant'

I couldn't believe it! Sharon Mason, the prettiest girl in my Sixth Form class, the most sought-after girl in the entire history of the school, had agreed to go to the end-of-term disco with me. I was to meet her under the Clock Tower and escort her to the disco from there.

I felt like singing as I rode my bike back home to get ready for the biggest night of my life.

I know myself only too well. I'm not the most popular or charismatic boy in the class. Having said that, I'm not particularly unpopular, either, unlike Martin Wells who is universally loathed by everyone, including, I believe, his entire family. I'm just there, a blank face in the crowd; Eric Gainly, that's me. Or Eric the Ungainly, as they call me behind my back.

I'm tall and clumsy, I've got bad acne and my face is pitted and pockmarked like the surface of the moon. I've got big jug ears that stick out from the sides of my head like satellite dishes. 'Prince Charles ears', my mother calls them, but that does nothing to relieve my self-consciousness about them. They're just big, flapping lugs; end of story. With a following wind I can use them as sails, hardly need to pedal my bike at all.

It would never have crossed my mind that Sharon could even consider going out with me – in fact, I've never taken a girl out before, have never been on a date and now I was going with Sharon Mason to the disco. Yes, yes, yes, yes! There is a God, after all.

Sharon has always, always, had boyfriends, right from when she was thirteen or fourteen. Peter Ablick had been her first serious boyfriend, when she fifteen or so. Rumour had it he was the first boy she had slept with – although as the rumour was put about by Peter himself, who knows how much truth there is in it?

Barry Nicholls, Trevor Speed, Wayne MacDuff and Mark Appeldore – all at one time or another had been a boyfriend of Sharon.

Lately, she had been going out with Jason Rossi, who had left school the year before and now DJ'd at the Viper Club, the only night-club in town. Jason used to be the school bully. I'd had a couple of run-ins with him. I can't say I beat him in the fights, but I gave back enough for him to leave me alone and look for smaller, easier prey.

In fact, I thought Sharon was still was going out with him, another reason I was surprised that she wanted to go with me, especially to the school disco. Hardly her scene at all, not when she could go to the Viper Club with Jason.

It had been her best friend, Kayleigh Smith, who told me that Sharon might go to the disco with me.

'You know,' Kayleigh said, 'Sharon really likes you, Eric.' I blushed down to the roots of my acne scars, feeling my ears glowing red like radiator panels.

'No,' I mumbled, 'I didn't know.' As far as I knew, Sharon hardly even acknowledged my existence on this earth

'Oh yeah, she really does, she told me, says you're quiet and polite, not like the other lads.'

'I... try... I try to be... polite, that is,' I burbled, sounding more and more like the village idiot every time I opened my mouth.

'She's not seeing Jason no more.'

'Oh?' I said dumbly, my conversational skills improving by the minute.

'Means she's got nobody to go with now.'

'Oh?' I said again, as quick on the uptake as ever.

Kayleigh rolled her eyes to the ceiling. 'It means, stupid, she'd like to go with you, so why don't you go and ask her? I mean, she can hardly come and ask you herself, now can she?'

'No, I suppose not.' I still stood there, my feet rooted to the floor.

'Go on then, she's in the library, waiting for you.'

'You sure?'

'Course I'm sure. Hardly be wasting my time talking to you otherwise, would I?' she snorted derisively. I don't think Kayleigh is waiting in line to become president of my fan club.

'I mean, really sure? You're not just making this up, leading me on to make me look like a plonker?'

Kayleigh muttered something which sounded like 'you don't need any help from me' before asserting, 'Honest, Sharon is waiting in the library for you to ask her to the disco. It's up to you what you do for me. I wouldn't go with you if my life depended on it.'

With that kindly parting shot, she turned and walked away.

And it was true! Sharon was waiting for me in the library. I shuffled over to her, my heart pounding in trepidation.

'Sharon... I was... er... wondering...'

'Yes?'

'I mean... er... the disco.'

'Yes?'

'I mean, would you... er...' this was it, the moment of truth and my tongue felt as though it had been tied in knots, '... go to the disco with me?' I finally blurted out, spraying spittle down her blouse.

'Yeah, great, why not? Meet me under the Clock Tower in Town Square at eight. OK?'

I spent so long in the bath getting ready, I almost grew gills. I washed and scrubbed and shampooed and flossed and brushed. I shaved three times, cutting myself under my nose and lancing open a couple of acne spots. I borrowed some of my dad's after-shave, about two tablespoons-worth and ouch, did that sting my cuts and acne as my neck flared angry red with razor burn!

It was raining when I got to the Clock Tower. I only had a thin denim jacket on which soon got soaked and I could feel cold rain trickling down my back. I huddled close to the tower, trying to find some shelter. I had caught the early bus to make sure I was in good time and I still had twenty minutes to wait until Sharon came. I hoped she had an umbrella with her. And a large, warm, fluffy, towel.

As eight o'clock approached, I started looking up and down the road, expecting to see Sharon. I peered anxiously at every car that came by; as it was raining, she could have got a lift. Eight o'clock came and went. I stepped out into the road to check the time by the clock, thinking (hoping) that my watch was fast. But it wasn't.

Twenty-past. Half-past. Twenty-to-nine. Still I waited, soaked to the skin. A minute or so before 8.45, a black VW Golf GT pulled up opposite. At last! I stepped out towards it.

The driver's window rolled down and Jason Rossi leered out at me. Sharon was alongside him in the passenger seat, Kayleigh and her boyfriend, Tony Mould, in the back.

'Waiting for somebody, Eric?' Kayleigh shouted.

'Got a date, 'ave you?' Tony Mould added.

'What a pathetic loser!' sneered Jason.

'Loser!' echoed Sharon and they pulled away, laughing like drains as they drove round and round the clock tower, waving and jeering at me. I felt totally humiliated... utterly mortified

And at school next day I could hear the sniggers, feel the looks of derision as the word of my humiliation spread around. Why me? What had I ever done to Sharon Mason to deserve this?

That was eight years ago.

I left school and went to university at Bristol, graduated and got a job in London with BP as a research chemist, every bit as boring as it sounds. I hardly ever went back to my hometown, certainly not to any school reunions.

But about six months ago I did go back to see my mother, who wasn't well. Afterwards, I drove into town to do some shopping. Town Square has now been pedestrianised, with the Clock Tower the centrepiece of a new shopping arcade.

By the Clock Tower, a girl was seated on the ground, begging, holding out a plastic cup. A dog, a black and white mongrel, lay at her feet. She was dirty and unkempt, her hair lank and straggling. She looked as pale as death, the flesh of her face shrunk into her cheekbones like that of an Egyptian Mummy. By her side was a bed roll and a plastic bag containing her worldly possessions.

It was not until I had almost gone by that I recognised her. Sharon Mason!

'Sharon, is that you?' The wasted creature looked up at me with dull-dead eyes. 'It's me, Eric, Eric Gainly.'

'Eric? Eric? Oh yes, Eric.' She rattled her cup at me and as she did so, her anorak sleeve slid back up her arm and I could see the needle tracks in her veins. The most beautiful girl in town had become a heroin addict. I could feel tears stinging my eyes as I put £10 in her cup.

'Sorry,' she whispered, her breath foul and rancid, 'about that time, you know?'

'It's alright, long forgotten.' It wasn't, but I still wanted to gather her up in my arms and take her away. But I couldn't and I hurried away, ashamed of my helplessness.

Some time later, visiting my mother again, I saw a piece in

the local paper. Sharon's body had been found by the Clock Tower, dead from an overdose, her dog still lying at her feet.

# A PERFECT JOB
## WEST AFRICA, 1987.

After being out of work for so long, it seemed like the perfect job. Well, to be honest, in my situation any job would be the perfect job. Things had been hard since I was made redundant from BJ Horner and Associates, an architectural practice in Sheffield.

At the age of fifty-seven, I was considered too old and not even the sniff of a job had come my way in the four months I had been out of work. Two interviews, just two interviews in all that time and there had been no follow-up from either. Most times I never even got an acknowledgement of my application.

We had mortgage payment arrears, our savings had disappeared, our credit cards were maxed to the limit and we were about to go under. The stress on Mary and me was intolerable. And then the recruitment agency rang with a job offer, a lifesaver.

The job was to take over and manage the Zunguna office of Dabakala Architects in the tiny West African state of Obaganya. I looked up Obaganya on the internet. It is a narrow strip of a country squeezed between Nigeria and Ghana, straddling both sides of the River Obagan. Zunguna is in the far north of the country, as far to the north as you can go, some four hundred miles from the capital, Obagan City, in the oil-rich delta of the river.

Mary was not so sure about the job, but I overrode her objections.

'The money is really good. Even after the local tax, we should be able to bank a fair proportion. We can get back on our feet again, put some money aside.'

'But is it safe?'

'Of course it is, it used to be a British colony.'

'Thirty years ago, maybe. Things change, there's been a civil war since then. And a famine!'

'Yeah, but now they've found oil. Oceans of oil. It's going to be the richest country in West Africa.'

'I don't know David, really I don't. We're risking everything.'

I did the sums again. With a two-year contract and an end of contract bonus, we could begin to get straight again. And hopefully, the contract might be extended beyond the two years. We could pay off all our debts, be solvent again and maybe move to a better house. I signed a copy of the contract and posted it off again.

After some weeks of worry, I finally got the confirmation from the employment agency and arranged to fly out to Obaganya. I would go ahead of Mary; she would follow on after a few weeks, once I had got things settled. The agency advised I would have to purchase my own ticket, something to do with currency exchange regulations which made it difficult for the employer to send the ticket, but the cost would be refunded as soon as I got there.

I showed the bank my contract, and on the strength of future earnings I was able to extend my overdraft and buy the ticket and $2,000 in travellers' cheques to tide me over until my first salary payment. (I had read that apart from the National Bank of Obanganya, credit card transactions are virtually unknown and nearly all business is conducted by cheque or cash.)

If you have a choice, I would suggest you do not fly Obagan

Airways. The Boeing 707 was old and dirty, the seats stained, and the only food offered for the entire flight was two hard-boiled eggs. A small can of local Obaganian beer cost £8 and 'Sorry,' the stewardess said, 'no change for £10 note.'

Obagan International Airport was a shock. Noisy, filthy and chaotic. The air-conditioning wasn't working and by the time I got to Customs and Immigration, I felt like a piece of steamed fish.

'You got pounds? Dollar?' asked the Currency control officer, who wore mirror sunglasses even though half of the lights in the arrivals hall were unlit. I had declared my dollars on the Customs form and wondered why he was asking.

'Yes, $2,000, in traveller's cheques.'

'Must change to Quiera, local money, it is the law.'

I had to sign my traveller's cheques and stand by as he disappeared with my money. After fifteen anxious minutes, he returned and thrust a handful of grubby, dog-eared notes at me. I counted them; at Q1270 to the dollar, I knew I should have got about Q2,540,000. I counted the notes again; Q2,385,005, about $120 short.

'I'm sorry,' I said, 'there seems to be some mistake. There should be more than two and a half million Quiera?'

'Commission!' he snapped, brooking no argument. 'Finished here, go to Health counter.'

I had had all my vaccinations before leaving England; cholera, yellow fever, etc., but my vaccination certificates were declared 'invalid'. I was fined Q25,000. The Health official put the money in his pocket and then stamped my certificates. 'Immigration desk,' he said, pointing to the left.

There, my visa was declared 'out of date' even though it had only been issued ten days ago by the Obaganya Embassy in London. Another 'fine' which, like the others, went directly into his pocket. At this rate, I would have no money left before I even got out of Arrivals.

I eventually found my suitcase; it had been thrown into a

corner and one of the locks had been torn off. As I picked up the suitcase, I was accosted by three or four porters, jostling with each other for my custom. I would have rather carried it myself except that a sign by the carousel read: *Porters must be used for the carrying out of luggage, Q25,000 for transgression.*

With a sigh of resignation, I pointed to the cleanest-looking of the porters and made my way to Customs. My bags were opened and a pair of trousers, a rather nice new shirt and my toiletries were confiscated as 'banned items'. I was too tired to argue. In any case, if I made a fuss, it would likely only have made matters worse. More 'fines'!

As we made our way of Arrivals, I was surrounded by a mob of yelling taxi drivers. 'Taxi, taxi, good taxi!' they shouted, jostling me, taking my arms to drag me this way or that. In the melee I lost sight of my porter. Somebody tried to drag my carry-on bag from me, but I held on tight. I was supposed to be met by my employers, but I could not see anyone holding up a card with my name on.

Then I saw my porter and suitcase disappearing rapidly down the forecourt. I tried to follow but was hemmed in by the jostling cabbies. My suitcase was tossed into the back of a car, followed by the porter and the car sped away. I shouted and yelled but to no avail.

I wanted to report the theft but the armed policeman at the airport doors would not allow me to go back in again.

'Go to police in Obagan City,' he insisted. 'Robbery take place outside airport, not a matter for airport police,' and he waved me away.

Then I heard my name being called and a short Obaganian waved a piece of cardboard with an approximation of my name, David Harrison, scrawled on it.

'Joseph, Administration Manager,' he announced proudly, showing me gleaming white teeth. 'Sorry not here before but the aeroplane was too early.'

'Early? It was two hours late!'

'Yes, too early. Normally it is four hours late.'

I told him about the theft of my suitcase.

'Yes,' he said, totally unconcerned, 'all porters are teeth-men.'
He had no idea how I might recover it,

'Police, I must report it to the police.'

'Police no good, police teeth-men. They take dash from you,
dash from porter but do nothing.'

'Dash?'

'Money, you know, for police time.'

'Bribe? You mean a bribe?'

'Bribe. Dash. All the same.'


Everything in Obagan City was crumbling. The roads, the buildings… it smelled of sewage and cooking. All along the roads into
the city centre, Obaganian woman squatted in front of stalls in
which nameless things bubbled away in rancid oil. The journey
was a nightmare of thick smoke, choking diesel fumes and
endless traffic jams perpetuated in a cacophony of blaring horns
and shouts.

Eventually, we reached the Hotel Splendid, named by somebody with a mordant sense of humour. I was to stay here until
my transfer to Zunguna.

'You must pay for room in advance,' Joseph said.

'Me? My contract says that accommodation is provided.'

'Yes. We provide, you pay.'

'No, no, no,' I insisted, taking my copy of the contract out of
my bag. 'Look,' I pointed out. '*Accommodation will be provided free
of charge by the employer.*'

In turn, Joseph pulled out a copy of the contract. In his copy
the words *free of charge* had been crossed out in black felt tip pen.

'You can't just change a contract like this; changes have to be
mutually agreed!'

'Yes. Yes of course, Mr Dabakala has mutually agreed this
change.'

'I will discuss this with Mr Dabakala when I see him tomorrow.'

'Mr Dabakala is out of country. Do not know when he will return.'

There was no point in arguing any further with Joseph.

'I come nine o'clock, we go to office,' and he climbed back into the taxi as I entered the hotel, trying to ignore the smell of something pungent wafting from a door behind the reception desk. It took ten minutes before anyone deigned to come and see who was ringing the bell on the desk. A man in grubby white trousers and a crimson bell-boy jacket finally emerged, scratching at his crotch as he did so. 'What you want, eh, man?' he asked grumpily.

I explained that there should be a booking for me arranged by Dabakala Architects. It was as if I had asked him to perform rectal surgery on himself with a blunt spoon as, with great ill-grace, he checked the reservations file before grunting, 'Room 240, Q33,000 plus Q5,000 late arrival tax.'

I paid the Q33,000 but refused to pay Q5,000 'late arrival tax'. I had only been in Obaganya for a few hours, but I was learning how things worked and I knew that the extra cash would go straight into his pocket.

After some argument, he finally produced the room key and pointed to the stairs. 'No lift?' I enquired.

'Out of order.' And at that, he went back through the door behind the desk.

When I got to the room, I found there were no sheets on the bed, the bedside phone did not work, and I was too tired to go back downstairs to ask for some. I rinsed my face in tepid, rather brown-looking water, crawled under the mosquito net and flopped exhausted onto the bed, too tired to worry about the cockroaches that roamed across every surface.

Next morning, I tried to phone Mary, but predictably, the phones were 'out of order'.

It was nearer ten o'clock than nine when Joseph turned up,

unconcerned by his lateness. I was to learn that time-keeping is a relative concept in Obaganya.

The offices of Dabakala Associates were housed on the fourth floor of a six-storey office block about a quarter of a mile from the hotel. Due to the traffic jams it would have been quicker to walk, but the heat was sticky and oppressive

There was a power cut in the office block, and I was to learn that the ONPC, Obanganya National Power Company, was frequently known as 'Often Never Power Coming'. When we arrived at the office after walking up the stairs, the receptionist was asleep at her desk and woke with a start when Joseph kicked the front of her desk. 'Blossom, show Mr Harrison a desk,' he said and marched off down the corridor. Blossom, her hair elaborately braided on top of her head (to demonstrate that she was too important to carry water jugs on her head like village girls do), reluctantly got to her feet, led me down the opposite corridor to an open-plan office and pointed to an empty desk in the far corner. Five or six draughtsmen looked up from their desks, sort of nodded at me and carried on with their work.

Nobody seemed to know what to do with me. I asked Blossom where Joseph's office was, but she told he was too busy to see me that day. I sat at the desk for the best part of three weeks, twiddling my thumbs with nothing to do. I was not allowed to see any of the drawings or details of any projects that Dabakala Architects might be engaged on, as 'only Mr Dabakala could authorise that'.

Nobody could tell me anything about the office in Zunguna, where I was supposed to be stationed, except to say it was very hot there.

When I did get to see Joseph, he would not discuss the refund of my air ticket – 'only Mr Dabakala could authorise that' – and nobody could say when he might return.

My Quiera were rapidly diminishing and I was forced to visit the Obanganya National Bank to withdraw money on my badly bruised credit card. Fortunately, I had negotiated an increase in my overdraft, but I was getting severely concerned about the situation. I did manage to call Mary from the telephone company's office (private calls not being permitted at Dabakala Architects). The line was poor and crackly, and I tried to gloss over my worries, but I could tell from her voice that although she was not saying 'I told you so,' it was implicit in her tone.

Robert Dabakala finally returned but he was 'too busy' to see me. Eventually, after another three long days, I was called into his office. He was a tall, distinguished-looking man with prominent tribal scars on each cheek, dressed immaculately in a dark blue suit with a barely discernible stripe, white shirt and dark red tie.

'What are you doing here?' he demanded brusquely as soon as I entered.

'I've come to work for you, to manage your Zunguna officee,' I stammered, shocked at his tone of voice.

'The job is cancelled. You should not be here.'

'Cancelled? Since when?'

'Since when I say it is. The University of Zunguna project is cancelled and so there is no job. You must go back. You should not be here.'

'I have a contract, a contract signed by you,' I said, waving it at him.

'The contract is cancelled. There is no contract.'

'I… I bought my ticket, paid for my hotel all this time… it has cost me a great deal of money to come here.'

'That is not my concern'

'What about my salary for the time I have been here, in your office?'

'If there is no job, then there is no salary.'

'My ticket, all my costs. What about them?' I was getting angry now.

'Recover them from the agency, they should not have sent you. Joseph wrote and told them the job was cancelled. This is not my concern.'

'Joseph has said nothing to me about the job being cancelled!'

'Joseph!' he shouted. 'Come here. Quickly!' Joseph scurried in, looking terrified.

'You wrote to the agency in England to cancel this job, didn't you?'

'Yes, yes, of course, Mr Dabakala sir.'

I could tell from his darting eyes that he was lying, it was obviously the first he had heard of the 'cancellation', but he was not going to risk his job on my behalf.

'You see,' said Dabakala, 'it is a matter for the agency. Take it up with them.'

'I... my accommodation costs Q33,000 a day for three weeks or more,' I demanded, determined to try and recover at least some money, but I sounded weak and defensive, without dignity.

'Once again,' he answered smoothly, 'this is not my concern. You are here as a tourist. Please leave before I call security.'

Joseph took my arm and practically dragged me out of Dabakala's office.

I never got to see him again. Or Joseph. The following day I was deported, as Immigration Police escorted me to the airport, barely allowing me time to pack my meagre belongings. My few remaining Quiera were 'confiscated' as it was 'against the law' to take Obanganian currency out of the country and the airport currency exchange bureau was 'closed down', even though I could clearly see it was not. I witnessed the police blatantly dividing my money between them and I was then marched across the tarmac to the plane.

Of course, the agency knew nothing about any cancellation of the job and refused my claims; in fact they were out of pocket themselves as Dabakala had refused to pay the agency fee.

Our debts were now crippling, and we lost the house. Mary left me to go and live with our daughter Sarah, blaming me for all our troubles. I had no option but to declare myself bankrupt and I now drive a taxi.

Mary and I are trying to reconcile, but it will take a while. But I'm hopeful.

As for Obaganya and Dabakala Architects, it really did seem like the perfect job at the time.

*Author's note: I did actually go and work in West Africa as an architect, but I am glad to say that our experience in Nigeria was very different from David Harrison's.*

# A FEW RANDOM POEMS

Some of these poems appear in my novels, others are just thoughts that appeared from time to time.

# WHY OH LORD?

I quite like kittens,
And sheepskin mittens
But snakeskin gives me a fright.
The mere thought of a snake,
Can keep me awake
Through many a sleepless night.

Oh how I hate
That bright banded krait
The rattlesnake, boa and asp,
I come out in cold sweat,
That one day I might get
Caught up in a python's tight grasp.

The sight of a cobra or even a viper,
Will make me quite hyper
When I think of that venomous bite.
And I'll dance a fast samba,
At the thought of a mamba
Sliding into my bedroom to fight.

And I will never ever,
From now 'til forever,
Get to feel any fonder
For the huge anaconda

Diamondback rattler, slim fer-de-lance
Sidewinder, Sea snake, Coral snake, krait;
Boomslang, brown snake and viper gaboon,
Bushmaster, asp and cottonmouth moccasin
Tiger snake, mambas; both black and green.

Vipers and cobras and all types of adder
And the dread Australian Taipan, the worst of the worst.
Oh why, oh Lord
Do they exist on this earth?

# ONCE THEY WERE FREE

Once they swam free,
Magnificent creatures,
Lords of the Sea.

Then,
Cruelly netted,
Dragged from the sea,
Beaten, not petted,
Caged like a rat,
Never again to roam wild through the waves,
To be kept in a pool,
Afraid and alone.
Who says that it's cruel?

Once they swam free,
Magnificent creatures,
Lords of the Sea.

Taught to do tricks,
Beaten with sticks,
Fed scraps of fish,

What more could they wish?

Swim round in circles,
Jump up through hoops,
Swim round in circles,
No room to swim free
Closely confined,
Of course, they don't mind.

Once they swam free,
Magnificent creatures,
Lords of the Sea.

'It's not for the money,
No, no, not at all,
It's for their own good,
To let them play ball,
It's not for the money,
How could you think that?
We're kind and we're caring,
(Apart from some wire)
But it's cruel to keep dogs
And it's cruel to keep cats,
So, set them all free,
And horses as well,
And when you've done that,
We'll still take your cash,
(It's in a good cause,
It all makes good sense
Lining our pockets
At God's creatures' expense)

Once they swam free,
Magnificent creatures,
Lords of the Sea.

And if one should die,
Well, never mind,
We've another,
And another,
And another one still,
We can bring one from Russia
Abu Dhabi as well,
(*To get one alive it's ten we must kill*)
To swim round in circles
And jump up through hoops,
It's not for the money,
It's for their own good.
Next year we'll bait bears
(They like it. you know).
Give us the cash,
We'll put on the show.
Excuse me, must go,
Got some dolphins to lash.

Once they swam free,
Magnificent creatures,
Lords of the Sea.

Set them free.
Set them free.
SET THEM FREE.!

Antidolphinariumist

# WHY NOT

Why do they
(whomever they might be)
Always say such things as?
Every cloud has a silver lining
Or
It'll be all right in the end
Or
There's always light at the end of the tunnel
Or
These things happen for a reason
Or
You've got to look on the bright side
Or
It'll turn out for the best, you'll see
Or
It's not the end of the road.

Why not
Just say
Shit happens. Live with it.

# THE BALLARD OF WAKEFIELD JAIL

The walls close in
Remorselessly crushing,
Breaking bones
Breaking sprit
No way out
No exit
NO EXIT

There is no silence
Where has all the silence gone?
The noise unceasing,
The moans, the cries, the curses,
The tramp of jackboots, the clang of doors,
The rattle of keys
Echoing around those dull stone walls,

My cell might be a prison,
But the cell does not
Imprison my mind.
Does not contain my rage,
Cannot corral my anger,

Injustice will not lie still,
Will not lay quiescent but cries out,
In tortured pain
Screams and screams again
Innocent
Innocent
INNOCENT

# WHERE?

Where's the fucking exit
Can't find my way out
Everywhere I seem to go
All the signs just seem to say
No Exit.

Life is just a one way street
An endless cul-de-sac
No turning left, no turning right
No stopping and no way back
No exit
No exit.

My dreams turn into nightmare
The exits are all blocked
There's no escape to anywhere
And the doors are always locked.
No exit
No exit

Trapped alone inside my head

The temperature is way below.
Thinking that I must be dead,
Can't find which way to go
No exit
No exit.

Where's the fucking exit
Can't find my way out
Everywhere I seem to go
All the signs just seem to say
No Exit.

# LIFE IS SHIT

Life is Shit
And
Shit ain't fair.
Who gives a damn?
No one else,
That's for sure.
Shit ain't fair.
But then,
Whoever said
It was meant to be?

# THERE WAS AN OLD WOMAN

There was an old woman who lived in a shoe,
She had so many children,
She didn't know what to do,
So she went to the parlour
And got another tattoo.

# GRANITE

Black granite crags,
jutting proud,
Stretching across the wind-racked moors,
On the backbone of broken dreams.
Dark-stern and forbidding.
The edge lies there,
Like the black dog of depression.
The endless wind whistles and shrieks,
Ancient ghosts who sense the residues of pain,
They are the destroyers of hope,
And slay the tooth of tomorrow's broken dreams
amid the ashes of yesterday's grief.
To stand on the edge,
Is to look down into the abyss of eternity,
Or look, look upwards into the blue void of nothingness.

# WHY

Once, not so long ago,
I was young and had hair.
Now, as quickly as the hair on my head
Disappears
It grows on my back
Why is that?

I used to have friends
Good friends
But they all fell away
Lost touch
Changed address
Round about the time I gave up washing for Lent
Mind you that was
Twelve years ago
And I have not washed since.

When in Rome
Do as the Romans do
Which means
Going round

Pinching bottoms
And speeding along the pavements
On a moped
Or Vesta scooter
Scattering pedestrians
In all directions

When in Rome
Do as the Romans
Eat pasta and dribble
Bolognese sauce down your tie
When in Rome
Go home.

Why do we call it
The United Kingdom
When we are ruled
By a Queen?
Shouldn't it be called
The United Queendom
Or
Does that sound
Too much
Like a gay bar?

What I did on my holidays
When I did not have
To go to work
Hurray!

Stayed up too late
Got up too late
Not feeling too great
Lounged around all day,
Watched the box

(Mostly repeats
or just awful crap)
And played my music
Exceedingly loud.
Which angered the neighbours,
Who live down below.
Well fuck 'em
Cos I'm on my hols
And why take notice
Of a man who collects dolls?

Drank too much,
Of extra strength lager
(the good stuff is Dutch)
Loads of wine
Red and white
And some rosé
Too

Ate too much.
Fried fish and fat chips
In a bag with vinegar and lots
Of battery
Crispy bits

Chow mein,
Egg Foo yung,
And Chou Shou Pork
Delivery included
Couldn't be bothered
To walk
To the Chinese takeaway
On the corner
By Guido's Italian
Cakeshop and Bakery.

Pizza came too,
In a soggy
Cardboard box,
And I think the cardboard
Probably tastes better
Than the thin crust
Thin taste
Quattro Stagioni
Which means Four Seasons
But to me
That means
Four reasons
Not
To bother again.

And that was
The first day
Of my hols
Tomorrow
I will really get down
To some really
Serious holidaying.
Anyone for a vindaloo?
And a bottle of rough-gut wine
Made from grapes
Trodden by peasants
Guaranteed
Not to have washed their feet
Since 1962.

'Hit me' it said
'Go on, I dare you.'
I looked down,
There it was,
Perched upon its tee

Like a budgie on a stand.
A little white ball.
Jeering at me.
'Go on, hit me'
Of course I
Was going to hit it,
How could I not?
Hit it
Clear across the other side of the world,
Or at least 200 yards
Down the fairway
(Avoiding the bunker sands)
With the length of graphite and steel
That I held in my hands.

It lay there,
Still and unmoving
How could I not hit it?
It was not as though
It was a tennis ball
Smashed across the net,
Or a rock hard cricket ball
Bowling down the pitch at 60,70
Or 80 miles an hour
It was just a little white golf ball,
Sitting still,
Waiting.
How could I not hit it?

I pulled on my glove,
(Only one hand)
Took up my stance,
Knees slightly bent,
Head raised, nose high
'Pretend to be a snob',

As the golf pro said,
A little waggle or two
And start my swing,
Slowly back. Arms straight,
Right wrist cocked
At the top of my swing
Head still
Driving down
Eye on the ball
'Hit me' it said
How could I not hit it?
And I did,
200 yards down the fairway
Straight as a die.
Tiger Woods?
Eat your heart out.

'God helps those
Who help themselves'
And so I helped myself
To 2 new shirts,
A pair of pre-shrunk jeans,
Timberlake shoes,
Underpants, socks and a baseball cap.

'God helps those
Who help themselves'
I told the judge
Who was not impressed
And fined me
Much too much.

Why is there no love in world?
Where everywhere is hate
Why is there no peace in the world

Where everywhere is war?

Why do people hate each other so much?
Where is the love,
Muslims killing Jews
Jews killing the disposed
Of Palestine,
Sunni killing Shia,
Shia bombing Sunni
Where is there no love in the world?
Sikh killing Hindu, Hindu killing Muslim
Muslim killing Hindu,
Christians killing Muslim
Catholic bombing Protestant
Protestants killing Catholics
Muslim killing infidel
Everybody killing everybody else
And all in the name of religion.

Why do the fat get fatter
Whilst children starve
In drought-scarred Africa?

And finally,

# BREXIT BLOODY BREXIT

Brexit bloody Brexit,
That's all we bloody hear.
Brexit this and Brexit that,
For year on bloody year.

And all those bloody pundits,
Who really aren't that bright,
Talking, talking, talking,
Talking endless shite.

'No deal' will be disaster!
'Remain' is just as bad!
But all agree, Theresa's deal,
Is the worst thing to be had.

It's a muddle in the middle,
That's neither leave nor stay,
But it will mean, hip-hip hooray,
The end of bloody Mrs May.

A second referendum,
The so-called people's vote?
But all that does is leave us,
In exactly the same boat.

So where's the national leader,
To get us out of this mess?
Well it won't be bloody Corbyn,
Sitting on his bloody fence.

Bloody Reesy-Moggy?
He's too far to the right,
Whilst Boris is for Boris,
Number 10 is in his sight.

And as for the rest of them,
Bloody left and bloody right,
They're not fit govern us,
They got us in this plight.

So is it time to pack our bags,
And head for pastures new?
But I don't think bloody Trumpland
Is the place to welcome you.

So we will do what we Brits do,
We'll stiffen up, our upper lips,
And moan about the weather
And the price of fish and chips.

*Annoying Mouse .*
*January 2019.*

**THE END.**

Dear reader,

We hope you enjoyed reading *Back to Basics*. Please take a moment to leave a review, even if it's a short one. Your opinion is important to us.

Discover more books by Giles Ekins at https://www.nextchapter.pub/authors/giles-ekins

Want to know when one of our books is free or discounted? Join the newsletter at http://eepurl.com/bqqB3H

Best regards,

Giles Ekins and the Next Chapter Team

# ABOUT THE AUTHOR

Giles Ekins was born in the North East of England and qualified as an Architect in London. Subsequently, he spent many years living and working in Northern Nigeria, Qatar, Oman and Bahrain working on the design and construction of various projects including schools, hospitals, leisure centres, Royal palaces, shopping malls and, most particularly, highly prestigious hotels.

He has now returned to England and lives in Sheffield with his wife Patricia. Amongst other works, Giles is the author of 'Sinistrari', 'Murder by Illusion', 'Gallows Walk' and the children's book 'The Adventures of a Travelling Cat,' all published by Next Chapter Books.

Back To Basics
ISBN: 978-4-86747-129-6

Published by
Next Chapter
1-60-20 Minami-Otsuka
170-0005 Toshima-Ku, Tokyo
+818035793528

13th May 2021